MAJESTIC CORPSE

Book Three of the
Emily Ellis Series

AMANDA JAEGER

MAJESTIC CORPSE

Copyright © 2023 by Amanda Jaeger

This book is a work of fiction. All names, characters, locations, and incidents are products of the author's imagination. Any resemblance to actual persons, things, living or dead, locales, or events is entirely coincidental.

Editor: Genevieve A. Scholl
Cover Design: Troy Cooper
Formatted by: Genevieve A. Scholl

TABLE OF CONTENTS

CHAPTER ONE...9
CHAPTER TWO... 16
CHAPTER THREE 21
CHAPTER FOUR 28
CHAPTER FIVE 32
CHAPTER SIX 37
CHAPTER SEVEN 45
CHAPTER EIGHT 50
CHAPTER NINE 55
CHAPTER TEN 64
CHAPTER ELEVEN 71
CHAPTER TWELVE 75
CHAPTER THIRTEEN 81
CHAPTER FOURTEEN 88
CHAPTER FIFTEEN... 94
CHAPTER SIXTEEN 98
CHAPTER SEVENTEEN 101
CHAPTER EIGHTEEN 106
CHAPTER NINETEEN 111
CHAPTER TWENTY 117
CHAPTER TWENTY-ONE 124
CHAPTER TWENTY-TWO 130
CHAPTER TWENTY-THREE............................. 136
CHAPTER TWENTY-FOUR............................... 143
CHAPTER TWENTY-FIVE 154
CHAPTER TWENTY-SIX.................................. 160
CHAPTER TWENTY-SEVEN 164
CHAPTER TWENTY-EIGHT.............................. 168
CHAPTER TWENTY-NINE................................ 172
CHAPTER THIRTY 180
CHAPTER THIRTY-ONE 184
CHAPTER THIRTY-TWO 189
CHAPTER THIRTY-THREE................................ 198
EPILOGUE...201
A REVIEW REQUEST...9
ABOUT THE AUTHOR.......................................10
ACKNOWLEDGMENTS 11

Majestic Corpse: A collaborative art game where people take turns adding and concealing their contribution

Memento Mori: Latin phrase meaning, "Remember, you must die."

Content Warning: Disrespect of Human Remains

CHAPTER ONE

Mills

"March Fifteenth." All it takes is two words and my entire body feels prickly all over. The Dignitary has given us a date. Finally, we have a date for ascension, full knowledge, access to the new realm.

The realm after reality. I know, I know. It sounds like insanity. Trust me, I would have thought so, too, weeks ago. But now here I am, ready and willing to accept whatever is next in my fate. Which just so happens to be something freaking big for all of us true artists. More shudders and shivers. It's unbelievable how soon that is.

My eyes drink in The Dignitary's steps in front of the room. She's taking them slow, giving eye contact wherever she can. Not that it's easy. Nearly everyone in the commune is here, smashed together in one room. When she drifts off to the other end, my eyes pull away. Briefly. Just enough to scan for Noland, the one person I feel connected with here. The one person who saw my potential and helped put this red band on my wrist, ensuring me a life of afterlife meant for true artists.

For the second time in my life, I thought for sure that man was dead. But here's the thing I'm learning about myself: I don't always know the truth right away, even when it's right in front of me. I'm okay with that. People are flawed creatures, and part of the human experience is learning that flaws are a-ok.

So, yeah, maybe I saw Noland's body stretched out on a gurney.

Or maybe it wasn't Noland at all. It could have been anyone else. Literally, any one of the hundreds of people who are on Memento Mori grounds. Besides, I'm pretty sure if there was a death on this commune property, we'd all know it. So I'm placing bets that whoever it was, was toted off somewhere for a little bit O' TLC.

I search the crowd for Noland. I don't see him. But he could be anywhere in this sea of linen jumpsuits. No biggie.

The Dignitary catches my eyes again with a sweep of her arms. Noland, my handler, my professor, will have to wait. Whatever The Dignitary has to say is far more important right now. I need to hear every syllable. I need to know exactly what to expect. I haven't been here for nearly as long as some of these Memento Mori members. I can't afford to fall any further behind in my knowledge or preparation.

"You have all asked for the exact day in which we will ascend into the greater realm, beyond what we believe as reality now, on this plane of existence. You've been eager and patient, ready and waiting for the right time to acknowledge when we can become our higher selves. Dali da Monet has spoken. I've heard Her. I've heard Them. I've heard it all. It's March Fifteenth."

Cheers erupt from the room. My own voice is blocked out by the deafening roar of hundreds of people. We're all excited, even those with a blue band. Or none. Even they have a place to help us ascend.

Even they feel the electricity of that concept.

Except, maybe a few.

When the roars die down, a few trepid murmurs break out behind me. The tension thickens in the air right on the spot.

"Dignitary?" someone calls out. A man, one of the handlers with a sad blue band dangling on his wrist. He looks cautious and curious. "Dignitary, we've all been talking, and there's a consensus."

All? I don't know who he's including in "all." I haven't been talking. Not me. I've been keeping my lips tight shut to myself. Who's talking?

I feel my eyes widen as my blood heats up. The way he's phrasing his words makes me feel like this man and whoever is included in "all" is conspiring against our end goal. I don't want The Dignitary, Iris Mori, to think I'm included in that.

No, ma'am. I'm done questioning the authorities who know better than me. It's time I sit back, take my place, and learn from those who clearly know better than I.

The Dignitary folds her arms across her, as if she's taking in this consideration as well. Since the man is behind me, her eyes are in my direction. Even though I know she's looking over my head and at him, I can feel them burning through me.

He clears his throat before he starts again. "The consensus is that we feel we're ready. As in, here." He points to his heart. "But here," he gestures to the room, "outside of ourselves … I mean, aren't there preparations we need to do? How do we get ready?"

The tension in my body melts away in relief. Not a trepidation at all. He's curious. And where tension just was, I'm filled with new interest. I'm curious, too. What do we need to do to get ready? What's going to happen March Fifteenth?

The Dignitary's arms unfold, and her face brightens up. "Let me explain," she says. Then, she waves her hands in the air, a silent gesture to ask us to sit. One by one, each person around me finds a place on the floor. I join them.

"Mori family, hear me out. March fifteenth is the next Supermoon. Each day before then, the moon will move closer, appear bigger. We'll have opportunities to bask in its warmth. Each night, it'll light our way just a little bit more." Her smile widens as do her arms by her side. "Consider it our path, our road to destiny. And when the moon is at its largest, that path will create an opening in the realms that will allow us all to cross over."

Then, The Dignitary lowers her arms by her side. She strides across the floor - her makeshift platform stage - and stops dead center. "But, yes, you're right." Her voice is lower now. And my ears strain to pick up every word. "There needs to be preparations. Which is exactly what we've been working on all along. Every project each of you artists have worked on is part of it. You've captured your talent in paintings. Pieces of yourself have gone into clay sculptures and paper mâché."

She slams her fist against her chest. My own heart feels its impact. "You've literally fed your heart to the beauty we've collected. You should be proud of that. You should be proud of yourselves."

The Dignitary nods her head slowly and taps her heart as if she's jumpstarting it with her hand. "Dali da Monet is proud of you. She thanks you for your loyalty. They appreciate your devotion."

Now her hands go behind her back and she makes the effort to look new people into their eyes. I wish she would do the same to me. I wish she would see me in the crowd, address me. I know it seems insane for me to want it. I've never wanted to be so reliant on someone else's opinion, but I do want her approval. I want her to sift through the crowd and really *see* me.

I want her to see me the way Noland used to see me. Talented. Special.

She makes her way away from me. She's seeing the special people on the other side of the room, and I wonder which color wristband they are wearing.

"And for those of you who continue to tirelessly work on our masterpiece show, I thank you. With every task, you ensure we will reach perfection. You, and our artists, all of your hands have helped to craft our final performance."

The way she says those last words makes my skin prickle in excitement.

"Each part holds a part of our message we will weave together, calling in Dali da Monet. And once our Supermoon night shines, our full message will be released to the public. Our message will be heard. Others will join in. They'll get a glimpse of our truth, the real truth.

And perhaps, they'll take the steps to be saved as well. We can only hope." The Dignitary clasps her hands together. "Our doors are open for them. For the people who understand the power of art and cleverness, and who believe our brilliant ancestors and the collective voices who collaborate to become the higher power - the highest power."

The entire room claps as well. Some people holler and whoop. As much as I want to join in, my voice holds back. My smile doesn't. My cheeks hurt just listening to Iris Mori speak.

"Once the public has had a chance to hear it all, those who have been chosen for The Circle will ascend first. We will have the chance to cross over, in our elite seats. Then, the rest of you will have the opportunity to ascend as well. I'll brew a special batch of my tea."

At that moment, The Dignitary picks up a cup of tea she had laid down on a nearby table and takes a sip of it.

"It's my special blend, but will have an extra bit of enlightenment included. Drink it on that day, and you'll have the chance to also excel to the next realm. That is, if you've completed your purpose on this plane, first."

She takes another sip of her tea, then lays it back down on the table.

"But like I said, the world is counting on us. The public needs our help to understand the importance of art and our souls. And as you know, the biggest impact we can have on others is to hone in our craft on materials we know well, as well as those waiting to be explored. I know each of you artists have your own niche you specialize in, but I can promise you I'm working on collecting materials none of you have had the pleasure to manipulate before. A set of materials have been selected for each of you. So please be patient as you wait for them to be prepared."

Materials none of us have worked with before? I take another look around the room. There are literally hundreds of people sitting in this room. How could she possibly know of a single material *none* of us have worked with?

The Dignitary moves in front of us again. This time, coming closer to my side of the room. I can feel her presence inching nearer and nearer. She lands in my direct line of sight. And for a moment, her eyes hit mine. I breathe in deeply, knowing this is it. This is the moment when our eyes will lock together, she'll give me a nod, and I'll know she sees what Noland saw in me.

For a moment, it happens. We do lock eyes. And I'm ready to absorb the next part of her message, feel her words swim within me. It's the closest I'll come to feeling Dali da Monet Herself. I wouldn't even know where to start calling Them in if I tried.

"During the Supermoon, we'll display the entirety of your crafts on a private server. Only those outsiders who have a predetermined electronic code will have access. We want to do our best to weed out the banals not worth saving from our operation."

Not worth saving? The little jolt I felt second-guesses itself. Maybe she misspoke. It happens to the best of us.

I study her facial expression, hoping to gauge what she had meant. But before I can read anything on the surface, I hear a familiar voice. Enthusiastic and slightly high-pitched. "And what about during? When we actually ascend? Will Dali da Monet simply accept us?"

It's Zak. One of the artists with the sad blue wristbands.

I watch The Dignitary close her eyes and fill her lungs with air. Her arms hang loose at her sides, then raise up to the ceiling. She stands like this, still as a statue, then without any warning, she yelps out loud and spins in circles.

Everyone else is quiet. Everyone else waits on bated breath. She's calling in the higher power. One of the ways she seeks to find the answers she doesn't yet know.

Then she stops. Both spinning and yelping. And her arms hang back at her side. The back of my neck prickles. I wish I knew what Iris Mori was feeling now. I wish I knew what it was like to know the highest power was inside me. I wish I knew how to ask for the answers I'd like to know, too.

"When She is ready, Dali da Monet will accept us all. Some of us earlier than others. Some of us in… separate ways from the norm. The Circle themselves will have a special seat reserved for their caliber." She bites her lip before addressing him again. "But as long as you hold Them in high regard and allow Her to speak through your hands regardless of the work or craft you have your sights set on, Dali da Monet should have space for you."

Excited whispers start to fill the air. I turn around to see Zak's response. His face lights up, and I can feel an electric current running from him to her.

Not me. My special moment is over. Maybe I never had one to begin with.

He's the special one after all. Iris Mori, The Dignitary, has found something within him, instead.

Again, I look for Noland, a familiar face. Nothing. I've got nothing.

Again, stuck between knowing what I should have and trying to figure out why I don't yet have it.

CHAPTER TWO

Livvy

The last time I was behind the wheel of Stark's car, he was drunk out of his mind and I barely had my license. Gosh, I wish that were the case now. I'd give anything for his beer-soaked breath to stink up the car next to me. I hate that I don't have a clue as to where he is right now. Or how safe he is. Or unsafe.

"Remember the rabbit hole."

That's what he told me. And then he threw me his keys before the circle of linen wearing creeps caved in on him. It was the last I saw of him. I didn't even hear him yell when a couple of those men grabbed his shoulders and whisked him away.

Who knows where they took him, but if I know my brother, I know he has a plan.

The rabbit hole. As if that's supposed to mean anything.

For goodness sake, Stark.

Sometimes I wonder if he believes in mind reading and thinks I have that power. Stupid men don't have a clue sometimes, and when I do see him again, I'm going to smack him upside the head, right where the fuzz grows back lighter than the rest. Because someone needs to smack sense into him, and if Mills has gone missing somewhere deep inside a cult, I guess she's not in the capacity to knock any sense into anyone.

I shouldn't say that. Girl is smart. Brilliant at times. I've seen the people who believe in… whatever it is they believe. They're deep in it, and so I remind myself that if she's brilliant and somewhere within a cult, then something that they've said makes sense to her.

I just wish it all made sense to me, too. So I can make it make sense as to why Mills is there.

Stark will get her out, though. He has to. Because, clearly, I'm not going to be able to do it myself. Not with the art Nazis gatekeeping information, and I clearly don't have the knowledge or skill to weasel my way in there.

At least not within it. But maybe I can still weasel somehow.

The tires rumble under the car as I turn down the graveled road. I may have kept my eyes clamped tight on the way to this commune, but my body remembers which turns we took. I just have to reverse the pattern in my head to get back to Stark's place.

Then what? I can't just go back to reality, can I?

But I also can't just quit the reality I've built. I'm not Mills, and I don't mean that in a bad way. If I quit school, I'll be forced to live my life as someone's cleaning lady or something, and I can't have that. My mind would go nuts at a job I'd hate.

I turn again, this time down a main road, and it's pretty amazing how quickly the mass of trees from that creepy commune fades into the background. It's like I'm leaving a whole other lifetime behind me. A dream of a lifetime. A story that doesn't seem like it ever existed at all.

And I'm leaving my brother and best friend stuck between those pages and down the rabbit hole.

That stupid rabbit hole.

Stark's car weaves in and out of traffic. I'm careful to only cut off the old men and ladies on cell phones. They're not paying any attention anyway. But every time I hop from one lane to another, I keep thinking about what Stark said.

The heck did he mean not to forget the rabbit hole?

Darting into the left-hand lane, I focus my eyes on the empty distance in front of me. I finally feel like I can breathe a little, putting the majority of traffic behind me just like the trees. All that's in front of me now is the way back home.

That is, until a blue truck speeds past me on the right-hand side. Some guy I no doubt cut off a little bit ago. And now he's out for revenge. The exhaust system sounds off, the gears of his truck switching with anger. A voice yells from the driver's window. I don't know what he says. It doesn't matter. Regardless of whatever is on his mind, I highly doubt it's anything like the massive weight on my shoulders. Jerk.

And then something flies out of his window, a white blur that flutters in the wind and smacks on my windshield. The piece of paper hangs there for a moment, blocking my view of the road. All I can see is this plastered piece of white, blanking out the cars and trucks and whatever vulgar things were being yelled out at me. And then just as quickly, it's gone. And so is the blue truck. The road is clear in front of me.

It was just a split moment where, yet again, paper becomes the center of everything.

Everything from the paper factory replays in my head. The smell of pine. The whirring machines. The weird game Stark played on a folded paper.

And… the rabbit hole.

That's it!

I don't know how I didn't think of it before. Memories are strange like that. Sometimes they get buried down and only dug up when something digs at their surface. That stupid piece of paper from the blue truck did just that. It scratched the surface and pulled out the memory of Harriet.

Harriet was our rabbit as kids. She was completely gray with a sweet, pink nose. And somehow Stark taught her every trick any rabbit could possibly learn. She jumped through hoops, ran through mazes, and even did her own variation of shake when he clicked his tongue.

But the best trick was the rabbit hole. Somehow, the memory was hidden deep down, out of sight. But the sight of that paper on my windshield dug the memory up and pulled it out into the open.

When Stark was feeling a little extra cheeky, he'd fold up a tiny piece of paper and yell for Harriet to go, "Down the rabbit hole!" She'd hop her little legs all the way down the hallway to my bedroom. Somehow, he even taught her to drop the papers and use her twitchy nose to scoot it in the slit under my door.

He always said blueberries were the key.

Some days, they'd come in droves. I'd be in my room, reading a section out of *Biological Abnormalities*, and out the corner of my eyes, little pieces of paper would scoot under the door. Within a few minutes, they'd pile up into a little mound. When I asked him why he taught her that trick, he said they were little bunnies going in their rabbit hole, and it was my job to catch them so they wouldn't run away for their tea parties.

I think he taught her that just to annoy me.

I always hated when he did that. Send in rabbit after rabbit, teasing me with the amount he could whip up and feed through the crack in a single day. Once, it was twenty-three. Every few days, I'd have another pile I had to deal with.

But also, I secretly loved it. I stashed every one of those rabbits into my desk drawer, little paper ears sticking out everywhere. I'm sure if I look hard enough I could find one of those leftover bunnies hiding somewhere back in my dorm room. Even after catching them all, I'm sure one or two escaped into my things.

The turn to Stark's apartment creeps up on me, and I swing the car onto the next road so I can park it and help myself into his place.

I may not be able to crack the same code Stark did to get into that place, but I've just cracked another. I haven't left the story of that place completely behind. I know exactly how I'm going to stay connected. Those rabbits are coming back.

CHAPTER THREE

Stark

You never realize how loud electric saws are until you're in a room with three of them going at once. And you never realize what contents a single body contains until you're in a room with one being dismantled in front of your eyes.

Books and movies can describe what's underneath a person's flesh, but it doesn't compare to what it really looks and smells like.

Every time someone pulls a saw away, chunks of meat fly in the air, and pieces of bone hit the walls and floor. I'm caught in the middle of the most nightmarish confetti in the world's worst snow globe. And Noland Elsinger, Mills's professor and captor, is being broken down into parts and pieces as the centerpiece.

I fight back the urge to whistle out loud. It's the one stress habit I'm well aware of and I get the feeling doing so right here, right now, would draw way too much attention to me. Attention I do not want.

All I want is to blank out the fact that this man's face is staring into nothingness next to me. But I can't tear myself away. Both because it's a job I've been assigned and because the fact is… this is a man.

Was a man.

And now it's… he's… a pile of gruesome jigsaw pieces that will never fit back together.

My stomach sours every time one of these other No Names starts up their machinery. Once that motor starts up, it's only a few minutes before a wrist or an arm or a finger becomes something of its own, completely separate from the rest of this corpse.

Corpse. That's what this man has become. Hard to believe he was ever anything else. Like a professor or an artist or anything humanlike. Every time someone else touches him, they take a piece away. Away from his body, but also away from his identity. Piece by piece, they chip away at who he once was, creating a future where he'll never be.

Days ago, he was a man, walking around this commune like anyone else. All it took was one coveted *enlightenment pill* for him to drop dead into a corpse ready to be taken aside and hacked away. They all talk about it as if it was a gift, something they all wished they could have for themselves. I hope I can get out of here before my eyes gloss over to be just as brainwashed as theirs.

The longer I'm in this room, the more the word corpse doesn't even make sense. The way everyone is treating this thing in front of us, it never was human in the first place. And now, it's just a thing we're breaking up for spare parts to be used to put life into something else. And, really, if I focus on my job and my job only, then it's barely even that.

Within the short amount of time I've been a No Name myself, I've learned that's how things are done here. No Names are recruited, sucked in with a promise to be a key source in the operation and a few dollars an hour. And their jobs are scattered into microtasks. Hundreds of men are given tiny assignments as parts of a whole. The Dignitary does this on purpose. Micromanaging everything down to how many steps we can take gives her the control she wants so she can have the status she feels she deserves. The makeup of work in this room is no different.

One man takes care of the arms. He uses his electric tool to hack through skin and muscle and bone, right under the shoulders. Another saws off legs in the same exact fashion. Three different No Names welcome the severed arms to disassemble the fingers and lay them out onto a tray in front of them. Little boney hotdogs ready for taking. I can't even count how many men are hovering around the abdomen, but I assume they each have their own organ to take care of in their own way.

Next to me, there's an assembly line. One No Name grabs a body part and uses a paring knife to make slits and skin off the piece into the most perfect flay he can. The next takes the skin and washes it in a solution that smells like hospital beds and disinfectant. Which, if there is any silver lining in this predicament, then this is it. It at least dims the scent of metallic blood and sweat that hangs in the air.

Then it's my turn. I take each bit of slippery skin and pat it dry as can be. When I was a kid, this was my job, too. Livvy would dunk the dishes in the sink to scrub them clean and I'd rub a towel over them to make sure they were all clear of water.

Only now, I'm not placing squeaky clean dishes back into the cupboards. I'm placing pieces of flappy flesh on a salted plate, only for someone else to hang them on a miniature clothesline to dry. Not quite the childhood chore I remember being asked to do. However, if it were anything else in my hands, I think my mother would be proud at how spotless each piece is before it gets hung up.

She'd Ooo and Ahh over each one, just like my plates. Pat me on the head and tell me I was a good boy. Thinking of it in those terms is the only way I can get through this without completely losing myself. And my lunch.

"Wheet-woo." I can't stop a tiny whistle from escaping. A few No Names look over to give me a curious look. I close my lips, attempting to stifle any more from leaking out. I don't want to let my nerves known.

Another *whirrrr* echoes in my ears and I block it out with more whistling. Not out loud of course, because I could go without questionable looks from the others, but inside my head. Surprisingly, my mental whistles do just enough to almost block out what I think they're cutting off now.

The head. His head. It's head. It's the head.

A sour churn in my stomach says my mental song isn't enough. I refuse to watch, so I focus on the task in front of me instead.

This one is a particularly large piece. I didn't realize until now, I must have already gone through the smaller bits. I lost count on all the finger and toe slices, but I guess I must have dried and hung up twenty. This piece in front of me is full of hair. Thick, dark hair that almost matches mine on my arms. I imagine the shape would match, too, if I rolled it up and fit it into place. Had Noland Elsinger been Black, it would have matched almost perfectly.

Amazing how when you break it down, we're all the same in some sense. We're all skin and hair in the end, made of all the same pieces, put together by the same color of blood.

"Wheet-woo." There goes my whistle. No; we're not all the same. Professor Elsinger was a monstrous serial killer. And I am a wanna-be vigilante, hoping to free Emily Ellis from this prison.

My towel dabs at it. I'm not sure if it's the size of the skin or what, but it definitely holds more moisture than the fingers. And the toes. But I suppose that makes sense. Our skin makes more oil in some places than in others. Maybe arms just happen to hold more than the digits on our hands.

"Hurry up," the No Name after me mumbles under his breath.

No one knows any of the No Name's names, but I like to think of him as a Jake. He seems like the type. The kind of guy who, in the real world, would drive a pickup truck while wearing a backward baseball cap. He'd drive to a parking lot to drink beer from a can on Friday nights while commenting on the last lap of the latest Nascar race and whatever trick his favorite car did to make it most invigorating.

At least, that's what his face tells me. In here, he's just like any of the rest of us. No backward cap. No truck. And the only circles that keep any of us keep going are from this cult's insanity, not inside a race car. We're seen only for our ability to fulfill a task, not for who we are underneath. Not our likes, our dislikes, or any of the intricacies that make us individuals. Our bodies are all covered in the same sweaty linen jumpsuits, and in this room, we are all now covered in someone else's death.

I wonder how long until we all lose our identities in here. Even the made-up ones I use to entertain myself. I wonder if making up names for these men is enough for me to remember my own.

"Almost done," I tell him while I dry off this slab of skin and hold back the contents in my stomach. Just by his gaze alone, I can tell he's waiting not-so-patiently to do his own job—covering it with a mixture so salty, I can taste it in the air.

I hope that's what I'm tasting anyway. My stomach couldn't handle it if it's not.

"It better be. We're already lagging behind on the tanning side of the room. Preservatives are way ahead of us, and I don't want The Dignitary coming in looking for an excuse for punishment."

Jake looks annoyed, almost angry. But, really, I know he's scared. The Dignitary has threatened each of us with punishment. And she's already proven to be a woman of her word. No Names get called out and never return. Whether that means torture or death, I'm not exactly sure, but I don't want to risk finding out firsthand.

So, I dab again. Make sure it's as dry as can be, and hand over the floppy arm skin over to Jake, where I watch him slather it with salt and hang it up on its own little clothing line.

For a moment, I watch it hang there, with the skin of twenty little digits hanging up next to it. Little pieces of human hide tanning under a heat lamp. I swallow back the bile rising in my throat. It's amazing what people can do when they put their minds to it. And even more amazing what we can overcome when we're forced to face something even our wildest imaginations never come up with themselves.

If you'd have told me a few months ago that I'd have found myself inside of a cult skinning a man after his death, I would have called you crazy. Only crazy minds can come up with that kind of morbid reality.

A nudge on my shoulder, and there's a new piece of my task handed over. Another piece, just like the other. Only this one looks like it got into a fight with a meat tenderizer. Shredded holes make it look more like a gruesome lace than careful leather. But I suppose that's just telling of who he was before he became nothing. Either a severely distressed man who took out his own feelings on his skin. Or—probably more likely based on the room I'm in and the people filling it—a severely distressed man who thought this was some form of artistic expression. Intrusive thoughts want me to stick a finger through one of those rips and see how big it actually is.

It's just material. Art material. For art. For art. For art. It's art.

A shiver rolls through me as I dry off the cleaning solution. Convincing myself that we're harvesting art supplies isn't difficult. It is what we're doing. Everything in front of me will be going toward some creative project. Convincing myself that it's anything similar to the paint brushes and canvas frames stored in boxes at the back of the craft store where I work—or, used to work; I suppose I work here now—is a little more difficult.

My finger does go through one of the tears as I'm drying it off. Some of the slippery solution must have caught on my hands and my finger slipped right in. And it stays there, paused in a moment with nothing but a thin towel as a barrier. Intrusive thoughts win today.

"Let's *go*," Jake urges.

And before he can remind me again of The Dignitary's promise of discipline, the door opens. As if summoned by thought, she's here. The

Dignitary is here, ready to assess our work and if we deserve praise or punishment.

CHAPTER FOUR

The Dignitary

Beauty. It's absolute beauty.

All my little men have done me proud. They never fail to surprise me, always one-upping themselves with how they accomplish their work. The good ones do, anyway.

And this? Well, let's just say we're working up to the Supermoon nicely. Everything is being prepared, and their careful hands have definitely done the majority of the work.

Well, the work I don't want to do. The work most of us don't want to do.

True artists have to save their energy for bigger things. Better things. More important things.

The room is gorgeous. Whereas the walls used to be boring eggshell white, they're now sprinkled with the perfect darkening crimson.

The floors have charming red footprints that have stamped their way all around the tiled room. It's like one of those old dance floor mats, showing where feet have been before and where they'll step again in the future.

Just. Beautiful.

And their clothes? Well, each of these men have tie-dyed themselves with the same sprinkling of tissue of wetness, proving that their blank canvas selves really are able to showcase their purpose. Had Dali da Monet told me there would be more availability for this round of ascensions, I believe a few of these men would be able to tag along.

But no. She said ten.

This is several too many. Allowing any of them in, even the new dark handsome one, would be a waste.

"Good evening, Memento Mori No Names!" I give them a clap to let them know I'm taking in the entire scenery. "We're only five days away from The Circle's ascension, and you all have clearly been working very hard. I'm proud of you all!" My voice stays cheery, excited. I have no reason to give them any other impression at the moment.

Especially when first impressions are so important.

"But before I release you from your current job and assign you the next, you know the drill. I need to observe your work, really take it in. As you know, everything you've done here today will be going toward a much larger collaborative piece." Though, each piece of material itself isn't nearly as important as the artwork that will be created from it.

The flats on my feet click on the tile. And even though I'd love to test out the sound when they hit one of those puddles, I take extra care to avoid as much of the bodily fluids as I can. My first stop is preservatives. Glass jars line up the shelves, each filled with a liquid Doctor James provided for us. Something made from pine sap or tar or something. I don't know. Doesn't matter as long as it does the trick.

The team over here did well. Floaty bits bob up and down in them. Some pieces I can identify. Lung. Heart. A bit of intestine. Others, I have zero clue.

Again, it doesn't matter. If it's interesting enough, my artists will know what to do with them. And you don't need to know what something is called to use it in art. You just need to know that you like what it looks like.

I like what this looks like.

A tall, thin jar holds two orbs that are staring back at me. Noland Elsinger's eyes. Though, enough time has passed where I shouldn't attach a name to them. They're no longer a part of… whoever he was. They're ours now, pieces and supplies to be resourced for something else.

They're just two orbs. Plucked from one source and ready to be used for another.

But they're not identical. And that's not right. One is clean-cut, completely rounded, and the other has a tail of… what? Nerves? Muscle? Tissue? I was never very good at knowing these things. But it has a tail.

I didn't request a tail.

I said to cleanly deliver all the pieces our artists could use.

This doesn't look clean. This looks messy.

"Who did this?" I point to the jar while addressing the rest of the room.

No one speaks up. No one claims their mistake. Every single blank-faced man is looking at me as if what I see in this jar doesn't even exist. I'm not stupid. Old? Maybe. Seasoned? Definitely. But I'm not stupid. I see the mistakes clear as day and somebody has to be punished for it.

Dali da Monet will not accept subpar anything, and that includes artistic materials.

I suck in a deep breath. Angry words aren't going to get me anywhere, not with this group of dummies who can't even carve out a pair of eyes the way I asked.

"Nevermind." I sprinkle on my best smile. "Even though it would be helpful, I don't need anyone to own up to their own work. But in case any of you need a refresher…"

I suck in my bottom lip to better scan the crowd in front of me. Each man is standing still. The thought passes through me that maybe some of them are holding whatever breath they may have.

Eeny meanie miney moe…. "You." My finger lands on a tall brunette with unsure eyes. His hands are covered in darkening fluids. They're probably sticky now, on the verge of drying. And he's standing over the thing that carried all the materials before they were harvested out. So it's entirely possible that the unsure-eyed No Name is, in fact, responsible.

I click my shoes all the way to him and can smell the fear and sweat dripping from his pores. It doesn't matter if he's the right guy or not. Holding him responsible shows to all the others that we need to take our jobs seriously around here.

The world needs us to.

Dali da Monet needs us to.

"Come with me," I whisper when I can smell his sour breath.

He shakes his head. No. No? That's not an option.

Then louder, I address the entire room, "Dali da Monet expects perfection. We cannot let Her down. Doing so would put everything at risk. Everything. For us. Them. The world." My hope is all these men feel the necessity in my voice. It's not that I want to punish anyone for the fun of it, no matter how fun it might be. It's that we can't afford to offer up less than perfection. "We cannot lower our expectations, friends. Not for anything. And so…" I lower my voice to a whisper, again. "Like I said, you need to come with me."

His Adam's apple bobs up and down. He gets it. He knows. And this time, he doesn't shake his head at all.

The room stays silent as I lead the responsible man out of the room. They all understand the point I'm making. They know we can't offer subpar materials, we can't go against what the Collective Voices say.

It wouldn't be fair to The Circle, and it's definitely not going to do any saving of any souls.

Let this be a lesson.

You can't fool The Dignitary by cutting corners.

CHAPTER FIVE

Mills

The more I look at her face, the more I'm amazed by the woman in front of me. Iris Mori, the Memento Mori Society's Dignitary, is a living legend. She's the kind of legend people outside of our community don't really understand. Or know.

And yet, she stands in front of all of us, in front of me, strong and proud. She knows her purpose here is to guide us along. It doesn't matter what anyone else thinks right now. Eventually, they'll understand, if they need to. But until then, she will quietly lead us through her meditations and knowledge, and her own self-discovery.

I found a pamphlet a little after earning my red wristband. It wasn't elaborate, just a picture of Iris Mori and a few paragraphs of a story. Even though it wasn't an in-depth read, her background surprised me.

No art camp, no prizes for her sculptures or paintings. As far as I can tell, she didn't even attempt a college degree in liberal arts.

But what I did learn is that she grew up in a single-parent household. *Relatable.*

And because of that, she and her mother struggled to pay their bills. *Relatable.*

When things piled up too much, they weren't able to afford rent in the two-bedroom apartment they were in. Her mother did her best to find ways to make ends meet, but it always ended with getting arrested for stealing or bringing home a strange man to share the bedroom with for a night.

The story then goes to The Dignitary feeling lost, jumping from foster family to foster family, without any real place to call home. That's when she decided to dump all of her emotions in chalk on the sidewalks and yarn around trees. If she could get a hold of it, she created with it.

When she aged out of the foster system, she had nowhere to go but the streets. That's when Dali da Monet first came to her. Drawing on the sidewalks, she heard Their voices. It shot through her heart and down her arm and created a chalk scenery that had passersby complimenting her with praises and spare change.

Dali da Monet saved her then. That's when Mememto Mori was born. A place for all lost artists to find peace and place, where the Collective Voices could encourage and save us.

To go through that tells me that she's an old lady with the strength of a Queen. And even though life has given certain tick marks that might slow her down—her backstory, poor eyesight with thick-lensed glasses, a speech impediment that makes her spit when she talks—there is nothing, absolutely nothing, that will keep her from performing and educating and leading the way she is.

One day, I hope to be just like her. Strong. Creative. And as all-knowing as a single person can be.

Possible? Maybe. Who the heck knows?

"Are you okay, Emily?"

She even cares about how I feel.

"Mm-hm," I answer, but I'm not exactly sure that's true. "I guess I just…" I take in a breath. I don't want to be rude to her hospitality. She came to visit me and brought her own calming tea to share. The same tea I imagine we will all end up drinking during ascension. Though the one she brought today doesn't have any form of enlightenment stirred in. It tastes like chamomile, Livvy's favorite. "I feel welcomed here, really. Everyone's been real nice. And this new room I'm in? I really couldn't ask for more. It has everything in it, including food! Seriously, thank you for that. Plus the fact that we get the chance to hang out and explore new mediums of art is incredible. I feel like this is where I'm meant to be. And even though I was a little hesitant at first, I'm all in now."

She takes a sip from her tea. Even the way she licks her lips after is regally impressive.

"Emily," she says, "most Memento Mori recruits are a little hesitant at first. They're not sure if they really want to leave the banal world, no matter how much the people within it have hurt them. But they always come around." She raises her eyebrows at me. "You though? You weren't hesitant. You were downright angry and unwilling."

"Mm-hm."

I was angry. I didn't think I deserved to be forced into anything, really. But after going through a cleansing and hearing what this group of artists' beliefs are all about, I understood. I wasn't forced into anything. I was offered a new start. Where people understood what it's like to pour your heart out on canvas or through paper and paste. Or through clay. Though, that last one was sort of a dud for me.

"But you know what I think that makes you, Emily Ellis? Strong. You're one of the strongest members we have, which means you have a special purpose that will benefit all of us." She takes another sip of her tea and swallows it. Almost in slow motion. Then, her eyes meet mine. "We all have a purpose here."

"Yeah, I get that." The words slip out of me. "But as much as I understand, and as much as I want to do my part, some moments it feels like, I don't know…" My last thought lingers in the air.

"It feels lonely?" She gets it. Spot on.

"Yeah."

"Emily. Mills. Loneliness hits all of us at some point. It's why most of us found each other. But it doesn't have to be that way here. You can choose to not be lonely. You can choose to feel differently. You just have to, you know, look at things in a different way."

Sure. I've been doing that my whole life. Or, at least, I thought I had been. But here, it's different. It's like I'm still unsure of where exactly I fit in. Even when it seems like I fit pretty perfectly.

"Dignitary, I haven't seen Noland in a few days, and he was the only person I could count on as a friend. Zak is, well, he's been busy with whatever project was given to the-" I almost let the words *non-Circle group* slip out. But I hold them back. I know how rude it would sound to label them as beneath me. "To the other side." That should suffice. "I just feel like even though I'm all in, I'm not exactly fitting, all. In."

She nods. She's been there before. It's why MMS exists in the first place. People like me and her and all the others looking to fit in, with love and appreciation for what we can do with our hands.

"Why don't you try fitting yourself in?" she suggests. "Go find someone. Someone else other than Noland, and get to know them."

"I don't even know where to find him if I wanted to." It's true, I'd been by his room and it's dead empty. Nothing but a spotlessly clean space, like a group of the No Names have cleaned and sanitized without a trace of Noland or anyone else behind. It's weird.

"So, forget about him. He's off fulfilling his purpose. You'll be able to do yours soon enough. In the meantime, mingle. Get to know some people. Talk with them. Share your beliefs and excitement to fulfill your part in the entire plan. You might be surprised as to what sparks fly straight from your soul if you allow it."

I finally take a sip from my tea. It's surprisingly sweet. And yet, it's also bitter. It's definitely not Joe's coffee, but I feel like the taste of bean water has disappeared from my tastebuds anyway.

This new tea might be my new drink of choice.

And if there was anyone I was going to mingle with in this whole place, it's going to be Paula. Time for me to make her my new best friend.

CHAPTER SIX

Stark

It's odd. Standing here in this room feels like hanging out with the boys. It's like a frat brother gathering or a special interest club get-together. Everyone is full of smiles and chit-chat, just socializing together as if we had been planning this meeting for months on end. Only, none of us actually had to do the planning ourselves.

By the smiles and laughter, no one would ever know we were knee-deep in sacrificial blood just hours ago. After The Dignitary left with her selected worker by her side, we were all given the okay to leave, collect our new clothes, shower off any of the professor we no longer wanted on ourselves, and now… this.

I find myself right now in a room full of men and all the comforts I could ever ask for. It's the perfect seventy-two-degree temperature. The LED lights are the perfect shade of calm. The furniture is plush and comfortable, perfect for our bodies to sink into after a long day of work. Tables are filled with platters of food. Drinks are in everyone's hands. Even the vases are clean and plants inside look like they've been freshly trimmed, like everything had been hand-selected straight out of a catalog just for this occasion. It's an oddly elaborate breakroom for a job that pays next to nothing. Well, nothing really. Even though we're told each job has a cash payout, I haven't seen a dime of it. None of us have. Not even those who have been here for months. Rumor has it that all the money goes into an account for us to access later.

So we're thrown to the worst jobs imaginable, just to break in luxury without pay.

Not that I'm here for the money. There's no amount of money that could get me to do the horrendous things I've done. No amount of money can make that okay.

It's all for Mills. I'll choke down any amount of discomfort through immoral acts if it means I can bring her back safely.

I sit down on a soft leather couch, next to a man with blond hair and facial peach fuzz. I'm going to call him Joe. He looks like a nondescript guy who would drink a coffee at Joe's, so it seems fitting. Joe offers me a platter of stuffed mushrooms on the table in front of him. It's only one of several platters of food, and if I didn't have the scenery of the butcher room playing in my head, it would all look appealing, too. I guess they want us to keep up our energy for all the work we're expected to do.

Shrugging, I reach for the mushrooms and grab a few on a napkin. They're deliciously creamy, full of cheese and lumped crab meat. And it's definitely not from a box of frozen meals. My tongue has memorized the tell-tale signs of freezer food. This food has none of them. I don't know who is cooking at this place, but clearly, they know what they're doing.

"What do you suppose our next job is?" Joe asks with his own full mouth.

I want to tell him I have no idea. I want to say that I hope it's something normal. Like sweeping up a walkway or collecting trash out of the quad. Something that has nothing to do with a dead body and hacking it away into pieces. I want to say that I hate what we just did. That it's inhuman to even think about such an act. I want to say that I hate feeling like I have to throw away pieces of my moral compass in order to redirect it straight to Mills.

But I don't say any of that. The hungry look in his eyes tells me that he's not playing the game like I am. He's in it for all the reasons he's supposed to be. The ones that have been fed to him until they wove into his brain and stayed there to call themselves beliefs. I look around the room and see most of the men here are the same. They're all chit-chatting away, making their best guesses and hopeful wishes as to what's to come next on their agendas. Whatever brainwashing has been practiced around these people has definitely done a number on them.

I choose my words wisely, "I suppose something is in store for us. Something that seems…important." I look to Joe for his reaction. He gives me a contemplative nod as if he's really soaking in the words I just said. As if they were an indication of something… important.

"Exactly. Next level important," he reiterates.

He reaches to another platter and pops a biscuit in his mouth and licks off his fingers. I watch a few crumbs drop on his newly cleaned linens. He plucks one of the crumbs off and licks it clean off his fingers. How he can casually eat off these clothes when there is no telling what was done in them last is beyond me. No amount of laundry detergent can erase the memories within the threads.

I know my own memories are burned permanently inside the folds of my mind.

I imagine a whole other set of No Names probably went in after us with Bleach and disinfectant, scrubbing the entire room wall-to-wall clean. The same group probably collected things like The Dignitary's shoes to toss them away and provide her with new ones. I saw the amount of blood that ended up on them. If she were to accidentally wear them outside of the commune and around anyone too observant, they'd easily link her to that Professor's disappearance.

Another guy joins us, helping himself to the spread on the table. Since he goes for the carrot slices, his name is Bugs.

Dumb, I know, but naming these guys keeps my brain from going numb.

Bugs chomps a bite off the end of the carrot and waves the jagged leftovers between me and Joe. "You two feel as lucky as I do?"

I'm not sure how to respond. Lucky isn't a word I'd use for any part of this. So I look to Joe for a clue. He laughs, so I give a chuckle, too.

Bugs bites down again. "I'll take that as a yes, then. I don't know, man. When she pulled that guy out, my entire body felt numb. Like, that could have been any one of us, right?"

Joe continues to laugh, but I go quiet. He's absolutely right. The Dignitary didn't wait for someone to come forward about whatever she wasn't happy about. She didn't even say what was wrong. Which means I don't know how to stay off of her bad side. So whatever this next job is, there's no telling if any of us will stay on her good side. Or if we'll do what's expected and end up pulled away anyway. Pulled away for…

I look around the room. Maybe the man who was pulled out was here. Maybe he was hiding within the group of No Names in a corner somewhere. Maybe I could ask him what happened when she pulled him out, to get an understanding of what punishment really is.

Don't lie to yourself, Stark. You know what it is.

"But we're lucky, we are. She didn't pick us which means we all did something right. Dali da Monet must have kept us safe. And if we keep it up, we'll be on our way to our own redemption!" He throws a hand in the air. I guess he's looking for a high-five or something.

Joe gives him one.

Joe believes redemption is for him, too, I guess.

Bugs's hand stays hanging in the air. "Come on, man," he directs toward me. "Don't leave me hanging."

I raise my hand up and tap his. I know I don't match his enthusiasm. But it's hard when you're not even sure what redemption means in this crazy cult world.

Bugs grabs another carrot and cracks it in half with his teeth. "That's what I'm talking about. Say, whatever they have us do next, should we stick together? You know, some kind of alliance so we can make sure we all make it in the end? Help each other and all that? Maybe share the money pot when we get access to it all?"

An alliance. Make it in the end. I don't like the way this guy is talking.

As if on cue, the door to the room opens up. I can even feel the air change. Judging by the way conversation has simmered, everyone else feels it, too.

The Dignitary stands in the door frame. And in her hand is a letter. I know what this means, and so do all the others. I force the lump in my throat down. I haven't had enough rest. I haven't yet forgotten the smell of death or the taste of blood in the air. I'm not ready for a new job. I'm not ready to endure that again.

Think of Mills. Remember you're here for her. Whatever comes next, if you're called to do it, you can. As long as you keep her in your sights.

"Attention, No Names of Memento Mori. Your new assignments are here." Her smile is wide. Almost maniac. "However, not all of you are needed for this job."

The lump in my throat pushes back down. Maybe I won't be a part of this next thing.

"Only three lucky No Names will have the chance to participate in this assignment, so listen up. If you're chosen, you'll walk collectively to the third room on the right. Inside, you'll find a small, wooden box. Assignment one is to pick up the box and take it to the display courtyard. Assignment two will be to open the box to expose the contents inside. Assignment three is to dump the contents in the courtyard in the designated spots. Each assignment is essential and must be done correctly. Should you fail, Dali da Monet will know, and She will come to collect you. Should you succeed, more funds will automatically be credited to your account."

Simple enough, I suppose, but the worst things can be veiled in simplicity. I'd rather not be called out for it. Besides, the least amount of work given to me, the more time I'll have to explore the commune grounds and find Mills. Maybe talk to her. Maybe convince her to leave this place and run away together. Get her out safely.

"So without further ado," The Dignitary folds the paper she was reading off of and tucks it away in her breast pocket, "today's lucky chosen ones are…" Her finger juts out in front of her and she scans the room with it as if it's a No Name detector, finding the right men for the right jobs.

"You," she points to Joe. "You," she points to Bugs. "And," I know before she even gets to me, I'm chosen, "you." There it is. Her finger directed at my eyes.

"Talk between you three and decide who will take which assignment. Keep in mind, assignment one will pay the most. Assignment two pays a little less, and the third assignment pays the least."

She gives a nod and a smile, indicating her own self-imposed assignment is done.

"I'm holding it," Bugs declares, and for a moment I'm not even sure what he means. But he starts moving straight to the door, and Joe and I jump off the couch to follow. We're not getting left behind. We're not going to be called out for not doing what we're supposed to. Not when we don't know exactly what happened before.

"Wait!" Joe calls out. "If you're going to carry it, I'll take the next assignment. I'll open."

Being the last to speak up, I'm automatically assigned the job that pays the least, and therefore with the least amount of respect.

"Which means you're pouring, friend." Bugs opens up the door and starts down the hallway, finding the third door on the right.

I'm having a hard time keeping up with Bugs. He's so eager to do what's asked, his stride is as quick as his mind is running. My heart races. My breath feels a little strained.

But I'm sure it's not just the quick walk. It's the question of what the contents are in a mysterious box. What exactly am I supposed to pour out into the yard?

We reach the third door, and Bugs opens it. There, in the middle of the room, is nothing but a white table with a single box in the middle.

"That's odd," Joe says. And he's right. It is odd. The rectangular shape of the box and care for the simple carving on it seems oddly familiar.

Steady steps take us to the table. I'd rather wait. I'd rather think about this a little more, observe this box and see if there's any other information I can gather about what we're about to do before we actually take the steps to do it.

But Bugs grabs the box without thinking. His fingers are already all over it. Again, I think about how many fingerprints have been all over this place, all over that bloody room, all over the dead Professor we tore apart. Including mine. I wonder how well the cleaning crew is wiping away each one.

"Alright, let's go. One last step," he tells us. So, we follow. It's not like we have much of a choice in the matter anyway.

I follow Bugs all the way down the hall, and Joe holds open the door for the both of us. Every one of Bugs's teeth show off in the sunlight. He's eating this up.

We make our way down the walking path, past three sitting benches, and all the way to the main courtyard, where everything is set up. Five pillars. Ten painted paper mâché pieces. Ten places for pieces of clay sculpture.

And several piles of what looks like dust or dirt. Oddly placed on the pillars themselves. No molehill would reach that high.

Then Joe unlatches the box. I hear a slight plastic rustling and a light scent of incense wafts over to my nose. When Joe hands the open box to me, my entire gut flops out of place. I know what this is. It's the same thing I remember going on our mantle after our pet rabbit died.

The same scent that scattered throughout our house when I accidently dusted a little too vigorously, knocked over Harriet's ashes, and spilled them into our carpet.

I hold my gut still. I don't want to throw up. My breath catches and stays put, too, and I do everything I can to separate myself from what I'm actually doing. Holding this box, tipping it over, and dumping it onto one of the pillars so it joins another pile. And another. It's not until then I realize there are several piles of ashes I didn't account for before. And I'm now taking part in whatever grotesque ritual this is, adding another pile into the mix of dirt. Dust.

Human ashes.

CHAPTER SEVEN

Mills

It's been a while since I've been down this side of the hallway. All the way to the beginning of the row. Standing outside of Noland's door, room number two, I wonder what he's up to. He's been shut up in there for so long, just silently… doing what? Conspiring? Waiting? Planning? Creating?

Dying?

Stop it, Mills. Remember when you considered him a cockroach? That man will never die. Will he?

Whatever it is, he's doing it alone. And as odd as that feels to think, maybe it's for the best. If the professor is in there meditating to call on Dali da Monet for himself, then maybe it's a good thing. He's fulfilling his own purpose in his own way.

That's what Iris Mori, The Dignitary, said.

I place my hand on the cold door, trying to feel the warmth coming from the other side. It's not there. Of course it's not there. It's just a door, after all. I have to let the idea go that Noland is the only reason why I'm here. He's not. There's an entire community, a family, in this commune. All of whom are here to support each other. I see that. I know that.

I just don't feel it yet.

It'll come. I'm sure it'll come.

My palm leaves the cold door, and I start to make my way down the hall just a few more doors down. Paula is in room four, and if she's just as lonely as I am, imagine she'll be excited for a visitor.

But when I step in front of the next room, with a large number three, I stop. Sound is coming from the other side. Voices. Not an argument, nothing alarming. Just some familiar chit-chat. The exact thing I feel like I'm lacking here. Damn it.

Chit chat. Banter. Friendship.

I lean in to hear it better, wondering if what's beyond this door is waiting for me, too.

There's a man's voice. Two, actually. Both sound deep and warm. It's as if they've known each other forever and they're just catching up over coffee.

How I miss coffee. I haven't had a cup since I've been here.

"A gift?" one man asks, and he sounds excited.

"A gift from Dali da Monet Herself."

"Theirselves."

"Exactly."

Loose talk has circulated the commune about gifts. Enlightenment gifts. There's a special one that's only reserved for certain people. I don't know who, and honestly, there's no way for me to know until it actually happens. But whatever that gift is, Room Number Three is receiving it, and I feel left out.

I wonder if whoever is behind that door will make their way to room number seven, my room, any time soon.

"It's for enlightenment," the first man says.

Of course it's for enlightenment. A stupid little twinge pulls at my insides. I don't want to be jealous, but I'm turning green right before my eyes. I want a gift. I want to shove whoever it is giving them out right down the hallway, to my door, so I can make sure I get a special gift, too. I mean, at least that would make me feel like there's something reeling me into this community a little more.

There's a little bit of rustling behind the door, so I can only imagine what's happening now.

Maybe the first man gave the second a wrapped box. Maybe he's opening it to see what's inside. Maybe his face lights up, knowing exactly what to do with the said gift as if it was built for him all along. Or maybe he's confused and needs some guidance on how to best use it.

More rustling. They're probably exchanging smiles and silent thank yous. I'm sure the second man is taking it out of the box, unlatching a lid, unscrewing a cap, and really appreciating what's left for him.

I'm sure whatever it is is exactly what he needs, even if he never knew it. The Dignitary has a way of doing that. Knowing exactly what fits inside the empty holes and giving the advice or gift to fill it.

"Thank you," I hear the second man say.

And I guess the gratitude is no longer silent.

"Dali da Monet thanks you, too. Enjoy your enlightenment."

There's more rustling, and while I know this is more formal than the interaction I'm hoping for with Paula, it's definitely closer than what I've gotten in a long time. Maybe these two men started as friends. Maybe they've exchanged pleasantries at first and moved onto banter. That banter grew into friendship where they'd share jokes and stories of their banal lives before the Memento Mori Society. Maybe, then, they were able to go deeper, share their beliefs, talk about their convictions, agree on the truths of what's all right in front of us.

Dali da Monet is the higher power. And He, She, They, are all above us, guiding our art through our bodily vessels.

It's weird, having a person you can share that deep understanding with.

It's even weirder not having a person to share that with.

The rustling grows a little louder. I hear a slam on the wall and what could be gasps, but might be more like whispers. Gasping. Scratching. Sounds that confuse me as crying. That can't be.

Footsteps grow closer to the door, so I step back from my stance and quickly move on to be outside Paula's door. Pretending to be interested in room four, I hear door three open up. One set of feet walk out.

A No Name. I should have guessed.

But then he closes the door behind him. I turn to look, and he gives me a smile and a wave.

As if we're friends.

But No Names can't be friends. They're just workers. They're on a completely different plane of field as the artists in our group. They don't fully share our beliefs because they don't fully share our talents.

It's a shame, really. They'll never truly be saved if they don't understand it on a level the rest of us are on.

But I suppose they're happy that way. At least this one is. He looks like a proud peacock waltzing out of room number three like that.

I wave back, and he silently walks away.

But it's not quite silent on the other side of door three. There's a bit more of that scratchy noise as if something is clawing the walls from inside. A few more whispery sounds follow. And then a slumpy *thud*.

I listen for a little longer, wondering if anything else is going to happen, but it doesn't. All is silent behind door three.

This time, I think about the last words the No Name had told him. "Enjoy your enlightenment."

Maybe that's what's happening behind that door. The artist there was given the gift of enlightenment. And now he's there. He's experiencing everything we've been looking forward to.

I'm shocked. Scared. Nervous. Jealous.

Why did he get to experience it before the rest of us? The Supermoon is supposed to open up the portal for us, and yet this man gets the lucky chance to experience it before the galaxy has lined everything up for it? That doesn't seem fair at all.

I throw my head back to the ceiling. I don't know if Dali da Monet hears me at all, but I talk to Her, Them, still.

"Dali da Monet, I know it'll happen in your time. I know I shouldn't be rushing it. But if you see it so, please help me to experience the same freedom. Send me whatever I need. Connect me with whoever can make it happen. Help me gain the experience and knowledge so I can reach the artistry level I need to be, too."

I have to believe the higher power has heard me. Otherwise, I'm not sure I have the confidence to do much of anything else in this place.

Sucking in a breath, I try to forget about what I just heard and all the jealousy that rose with it. And, instead, I knock on door number four.

This could very well be the next step that Dali da Monet has for me. Friendship. With Paula. And our shared notions of what's in store for us as Mori members. Maybe if we can prove our devotion and understanding together, we can experience the gift of enlightenment together, too.

CHAPTER EIGHT

Livvy

"Woo-sahh." I know Joe's is known for its coffee, but a cup of chamomile and honey is exactly what I need to wake up and figure out what the hell my next step will be.

Remember the rabbit hole.

I got it, Stark. I remember. But I can't exactly drop paper notes over the locked iron gate in the middle of pine woods and hope no one else picks them up before him, right? Or can I?

Maybe I need a secret code. Maybe I -

"Hey, Olivia."

I look up to a beaming blonde. Mariëtte Dunn. The same Mariëtte I thought was a weird sorority sister, forcing girls to swallow their emotions and follow her to the end of the earth blindly. She's also the same girl who proved me wrong by showing Mills what she was actually up to: training her sorority self-defense from the kind of jerks who like to take advantage of girls who appear to be weird sorority sisters.

The kind of jerks like the professor Mills looked up to. I sure hope he gets what's coming to him, eventually. If he hasn't already met his fate.

"Hey Mariëtte. Have a seat?" I offer up the chair in front of me. Before she sits down, she tips it back, inspects it, and digs out a cloth from her Alpha pink jumper to dust it off.

Okay, maybe she's not a weird sister, but she is a particular one.

"So, you ready to strategize?"

I nod. Yup. As much as I need to focus on Stark and our communication, I'm also smack dab in the middle of something else I need to focus on. Something that might be even more stressful, for most undergraduate college students anyway: Partner science projects.

"Do you have any thoughts?" I already do, but it's the polite thing to ask. Especially when my thoughts are a little scrambled.

Mariëtte is a psychology major. I'm doubling in biology and chemistry. It just so happens that Volga University is offering a special three-week workshop that will give both of us an extra three credits toward our degrees. It's called: The Art of Brain Chemistry. And our assignment is to come up with a way to study the brain through chemical stimulation. Complete it, and we're one step closer to both of our degrees.

She shrugs. "I could ask one of my sisters if we could study her? We could do a before and after with a week's worth of workouts? We could test her sweat or measure blood samples and measure them up against the good workouts and the ones that aren't so great."

I think about asking an Alpha girl if we could study her for three weeks. *"Can we put you through an even more rigorous training session than normal and take some of your blood samples to see if your body chemistry has changed?"* Even if Mariëtte asked nicely, I'm not so sure that would be the best way to spend our time. If it were me, I wouldn't want someone judging my blood samples for a grade. No; we need something a little different.

I shake my head. "I'm not sure we should study a person, Mariëtte. It doesn't feel right to me."

She considers it for a moment, then flips her wrist in the air. "Well, then I'm all out of ideas. You got anything better?"

Remember the rabbit hole.

"Rabbits." The world slips out as easily as the thought passes through me.

"Okay… rabbits?" Mariëtte's eyebrows hitch up.

"Sure, rabbits," I address her, but my own eyes look down while I focus on what exactly would pass for the assignment. And for what I need. "Well, maybe one rabbit."

My memory conjures up an image of a grey bunny with a twitchy pink nose. "When my brother and I were little, we had a rabbit, Harriet. When Stark first brought her home, I thought she'd be boring. You know, hang out in the corner of a room and eat carrots and stuff. Rabbits weren't exactly my favorite animal. I wanted a dog. Something I could train to do whatever I wanted at a click or a whistle."

I look back up at Mariëtte. Her eyebrows have calmed themselves down. She's listening, following my train of thought.

"But she was actually pretty cool. Stark wanted to prove to me that she was just as good as any dog. And he did. He was able to teach her a few tricks. Whenever he'd say, 'Down the rabbit hole!' she would run to my room and drop whatever was in her mouth at my door. Sometimes, Stark would give her a little origami rabbit and it was like she was dropping off her own bunnies for me to take care of."

I can feel the corners of my mouth turn up at the memory.

"So, you want to use this project to get yourself a pet rabbit like your Harriet?"

If only that was the case. I'd only have the pressure of a grade on my shoulders. "Not exactly. But I was thinking we could test what happens chemically to a rabbit when you train one to do… different tricks."

"Like dropping off paper bunnies?"

"Down the rabbit hole."

Mariëtte lifts her hand in the air to flag down a waitress. While I hear her order a water, I try to come up with a way I could create my own rabbit hole, straight to Stark.

"So, what's your hypothesis, Olivia? What chemically happens to a rabbit when it takes paper bunnies to some kind of," she waves her hand in a circle, "metaphorical rabbit hole?"

I chuckle, because that was the fun part about Harriet, the rabbit. "Well, it's not so much about carrying pieces of paper. Or ringing a bell. Or jumping through hoops. Or any of that."

"Your rabbit jumped through hoops?" She barks out a laugh. "That, I've gotta see."

"I'm telling you, she did a lot of really awesome things. But chemically, I'm willing to bet nothing much happened while doing the trick. It's more like what happens before and, well, after."

"After? Like, a reward?"

"Specifically, blueberries."

The waitress arrives at our table with Mariëtte's water, complete with a large wedge of lemon hanging on the glass rim.

"Blueberries were her favorite. Every time we offered one to her, she'd follow Stark to do anything. Before long, she figured out the trick, and she'd do it without fail. As long as there were blueberries involved, she followed any direction he gave."

Mariëtte takes a sip of her water, and mentally, I'm preparing for Harriet Number Two and a buttload of blueberries lining up to Blackwell Avenue so she can find her way to Stark. It's just a matter of figuring out how to train this currently non-existent rabbit to do even more than that. Like actually finding Stark. And dropping it at his feet so that no one else will snatch it up and read my messages.

"So you think that blueberries have, what, some kind of chemical in them?"

"Nah. Not the blueberries themselves." Though, that might be an interesting thing to look into later. "But in the rabbit. You know how when you eat a slice of cake or a bowl of ice cream? That first bite is so much better than the rest and it makes you want to go after it again and again. I'm willing to bet that the same oxytocin is in play."

"Ah, the love hormone."

"Exactly. My hypothesis is that oxytocin levels spike whenever a rabbit gets something delicious, like a blueberry. But if we train its brain to understand what we're asking of it-"

"Like a trick-"

"Then maybe the levels of oxytocin spike even higher. The higher the levels, the more likely the rabbit will work for it." And I need this rabbit to work hard.

Mariëtte pinches the lemon wedge between her fingers and squeezes the juice into her water. A few drops fly from it and land on the napkin by my tea. I watch the spots darken, and within seconds those spots disappear. Never to be seen again.

No, not never.

The pieces start fitting together before I can even get the thoughts straight. With one hand, I pick up the napkin with the dried lemon specks. With the other, I run my hand over the top of my tea. Still hot. Steaming hot. Perfect.

I place the napkin over the top, allowing the steam to dampen and heat it up. Like a charm, the lemon spots darken up. Exactly what I expected.

"So I guess we're getting ourselves a rabbit, huh?"

I nod. Smile. We're getting a rabbit.

And with a little bit of luck, I'll be able to communicate with Stark again.

CHAPTER NINE

Mills

Of course. A jug. Now that I see what Paula made out of her clay, it makes complete sense as to what should be made with the material. I should have tried to put together a piece of pottery. A vase or bowl or something. Something that made sense. At least more sense than a wonky butterfly.

My clunky piece looks so sad next to her elaborate detailed jug. Filigree decorates the base, two handles almost look like lace, and the lip of the jug is like something out of a Frances Broomfield painting. I shouldn't compare my work next to hers. It's not fair to either of us. We are part of The Circle, after all. We're supposed to be the best of the best. And I know if I were to even think that I'm not good enough too loudly, The Dignitary, Iris, might take that position away from me.

So I'll shut up and accept that I created what I did and so did she. We'll both end up in the same place regardless. Our red wristbands have already determined where we're going.

"You're very good with clay," I tell her while leaning against her bed. So this is what community feels like. Hanging out in someone else's room to talk. About our likes, our dislikes. The projects we are working on. What to expect later. Only, the concerns I really have are kept silent. And instead of matching Greek colors, we're in the same linen jumpsuits.

This is friendship, right? This is what I've been missing while on commune grounds.

Just working to the common goal of ascending to the next realm while expanding our knowledge and talents while we find our purpose in the realm of reality.

No big.

I know what my purpose is. And judging by Paula's work, I know hers is the same. We're supposed to reach the world through our art, to unlock a portal to where our souls will be welcomed. Where we'll finally be able to reach the same level of enlightenment as Van Gogh and Picasso and Munch and every other great in our past and future.

Sometimes, I also wonder what Zak is doing, and how the non-Circle members will fulfill their own purpose for our ascension, and it makes me sad. My understanding is that their souls will stay here. No matter how much they try to improve their skills now, they haven't been chosen. They're not part of the final plan, even if they drink the tea of enlightenment during the Supermoon. Sad, really.

I'm so thankful I'm in The Circle. Next to Paula.

"Thanks." Paula tucks a piece of her strawberry-red hair behind her ear and gives me a shy smile. "It's just a water jug, though."

But it's not just a water jug. It's beauty. It's solid. Every single detail was purposefully created. It's clear she was able to meticulously craft each section as if her entire heart depended on bringing it to life in the most perfect way, or else it would stop beating. It's the exact thing I wish I could create with my hands.

"Paula, this is exceptional. It's really no wonder why you are part of the chosen."

With my sad, sinking butterfly, I have to wonder why I was, though. How do I not know how to handle such a material? Am I doomed to only be a painter? Could I ever be a master artist who can work with any material to create anything her heart desires? What does that mean if I can't? Maybe it was a misunderstanding. Maybe I should have been thrown off to the side with Zak and the other blue wristband, non-Circle members.

Just when I'm about to ask Paula for tips on how to handle three-dimensional materials, there's a knock on the door. We look at each other and wonder if this is it. If we're about to be given the next task, another project to work on, showcase ourselves within our art so that Dali da Monet can welcome us into the next realm.

Or enlightenment.

Where we're all waiting to be saved.

So the world can be saved.

I think that's how this whole thing is going. And every minute I spend being with Paula and the others enforces my growing belief.

I know, strange to come from a girl who's never really known much of beliefs beyond a simple moral compass. But here we are.

Paula tentatively gets up from her seat as there's another knock at the door. Whatever is waiting for us, it must be important. It would have been nice if, you know, whoever is on the other side of the door would have allowed enough time for two girls from the opposite side of the wall to actually make their way to the door.

There's a third knock when Paula finally answers. When she opens the door, two faces smile back at her. One, with a hand hovering in midair as if he was in the middle of his next knock. This No Name is clearly the impatient one.

"Oh good. I'm glad you answered," he tells us with his lips pulled back from his teeth. "We're here to collect your latest contributions."

Paula looks down at the floor, clearly not wanting to hand over her work, yet. I don't blame her. Something of that caliber deserves to be held and loved for more than just a few days.

One look at the second man at the door tells me it doesn't matter. They're here for our art, and it's our job to give it to them. The way the both of them are scrutinizing us and the room, I get the feeling neither will leave without our clay sculptures in their hands.

Then again, they're collecting them for MMS's final showcase. The display on Supermoon day, where we will call onto Dali da Monet, drink our tea, become enlightened and save the world.

"Wait here," I tell them, and leave to go fetch my butterfly. The way the wings flop over under their own weight is another reminder that there's a lot I don't know. There's a huge missing piece of knowledge and experience that's preventing me from perfection. The freedom I felt while creating it was temporarily lived. But it was there. And if I focus enough, I'll be able to release my full talent to the world.

With two hands, I carry my not-so-delicate butterfly to the front door. "Here." I hand it over to the eager man. "Here's my contribution."

He sniggers as if his judgment matters. I know it doesn't. It's not his judgment that actually determines anything of the future realm. I don't have to impress this guy or the man next to him. The No Names are just that. No Names. Their opinions aren't the ones that matter. Not in the end.

I just have to impress Dali da Monet. The genius collective. The voice of reason and expression that guides us all in Memento Mori. No pressure or anything.

"We need yours, too." The second No Name points to Paula. His tone is kinder. He's doing his job, but he's not pushing us too rough. "We'll wait here."

Strange men, these No Names are.

Paula nods and she tentatively leaves her stance by the door to find her jug. The way her face falls, I know she's as uncertain of her work's future as I am of my own work's present.

While the three of us wait, I take note of these two men. From where I stand, they seem like two perfectly normal men. They're both nondescript, tall and broad. They probably both came into MMS with the same lost feeling, unsure of what their purpose on this earth is. They probably came to Iris Mori, confused as to who they are, looking for a family who could take them in and give them a purpose they can feel proud of.

Men who have lost their families. Men who have left their jobs. Men who couldn't find one step to take after another, who couldn't see what a future might hold because the realm of reality had given them reason to believe there was no future with their name on it.

It's a good thing they found us, our family of artists. Because these two men and all the others like them now have purpose that makes sense. They have the job to do what needs to be done so that artists can save our communities with our views and talents.

They're both keeping their stance strong. They're both ready and willing to take care of the request they were given. They probably both found their way to MMS loosely interested in art before they found our truths in what's waiting for us all on the other side of so-called reality. Again, it's a good thing they found their way here. Anyone who can experience a little of the truth before they either move onto the better or get sucked up into reality is another person who can help spread the messages we have.

The eager No Name clicks his tongue impatiently and taps his foot. I'm glad he's not the one holding my clay butterfly. I wouldn't want him to squeeze his fist and accidentally squash it. Even though it's not the most elaborate creation, I still don't want to see it destroyed. It has potential, if you just give it a little love.

She finally comes back with her clay piece in hand. With the slightest amount of hesitation, Paula offers up her jug with both hands. "Here," she almost whispers. "This is for Dali da Monet."

My mouth pulls upward. I'm so proud of her. I know there's a part of her who doesn't want to give it up. But there's something so much bigger awaiting her by handing it over.

The eager man chuffs and takes the jug from her without waiting. He's more interested in his job than in the actual craftsmanship of what he's holding. I swear if he drops it, I'll go all Alessandro Magnasco on his ass. Why does he have to act like it's trash in his hands?

A lump forms in my throat. I know we're here to catch the eye of the collective voice, Dali da Monet. I know we're here for bigger things than what we were always told were big for us before Memento Mori was placed into our lives. I know we're here for a bigger purpose than ourselves.

But something about the way this guy holds Paula's perfect pitcher makes me see red. Isn't part of our purpose to reach others? The banals? To translate the messages of our artistic ancestors in a way that can be consumed by those who aren't artistically inclined?

Aren't we supposed to save the world through our art? Through pieces of our souls? One by one, aren't we supposed to reach them with our messages so more can ascend? And so those who can't can fulfill their purpose here, in this reality?

Wouldn't that mean we need to create images and pieces that would speak to everyone? Including these two men at Paula's door?

They nod their thanks and leave without any goodbye. This solidifies my thoughts. Holding something so precious deserves more than a nod. They should have oohed and ahhed. They should have felt the power of her talent with a single touch. "Paula, did you see how they acted?"

She bites her bottom lip. "They were excited. But not for our clay pieces."

"Exactly." She sees it, too. "Isn't our entire purpose here to move people through our talents? Aren't we supposed to get people excited about art? So they can find meaning, and all that? Aren't we supposed to save the world through our art?

She nods. "Yeah. That's what The Dignitary says."

"Not just The Dignitary. Our handlers told us that, too, right? Isn't that the message from the higher power? Isn't it what we're all agreeing on?"

Paula is silent, but I know she agrees. Everyone who's a part of this community has heard that message time and time again. It's just now that the two of us are starting to realize what that could mean for us. Now. Here.

We could take things into our own hands.

"But, Paula, how are we supposed to save the world when not even these two No Names understand it?"

"What do you mean, Mills?" Paula looks like she's going to throw up; her pale skin shines with worry.

"I mean, let's do something. Let's take our own initiative to start with those who are right here."

"You mean, save them first?"

This is what friendships are made of.

"Exactly. You and me, we can do it. We just have to come up with a project that will move everyone on the commune, including the No Names who take their job more seriously than their purpose."

The question then becomes what and where. We could do something in our rooms, hide it away from everyone, and do a big reveal to the rest of the commune. That at least worked for shock value when I did that on Volga's campus.

A chuckle escapes at the memory.

But I'm afraid that might take away from the big reveal being planned by The Dignitary herself. I'm not exactly sure how it's all going to go down, but I know it's the reason why the No Names showed up at Paula's door asking for our clay. And if we take away from what's planned, then there's no telling what kind of punishment we may have to endure. We might not be allowed into the next realm. How devastating would that be?

No; we need to do something that would add to what's planned.

Every bit of art we're asked to do is taken to a single, predetermined place: the quad. The yard. The community land. Whatever you want to call it. It's a little field of grass with pedestals to display what we've created so far. At some point, the collection will be revealed to the public, and we'll all see what future awaits us, either eventual ascension and awakening or boring-old-wait-and-see.

We don't yet know how it's going to be revealed. And as far as I can tell, no one in The Circle has been notified of those details. But once everything is revealed, it's going to be stunning. And the world will finally understand what lives in the heart of an artist. Of all artists.

So, I can't take away the limelight of The Dignitary. I'm pretty sure that would mean devastating consequences for me. For all of us. Something like shame and embarrassment, but ten-fold. We need to come up with something out in the open. No big reveal. No song and dance number. Just a good old-fashioned live artwork for The Circle, the No Names, The Dignitary, and everyone else in this commune can appreciate as they pass it by and take it in.

As if Paula has read my mind, she says, "Mills, you know where they're collecting everything? Out on that field? What if we painted the retaining wall around it?"

Perfect.

"Perfect! It'll be our own addition to the collection. It'll add to the creativity that's already there. And it'll mean even more because we're choosing to do it. Paula, you're brilliant."

Her smile is all I need to know she knows it, too. Together, we help ourselves to the cabinets. We already know where the paints and brushes are, so we scramble to collect as many as we can.

Jars of marmalade red and lemongrass green come falling into our hands. Each one feeds my excitement. And if only Noland could see me now, grabbing at every paint willingly and eagerly to test our limits and share a piece of ourselves. I'm sure he would be proud of me.

I'm ready to become a little closer to the next realm, too. I can't wait to see the looks on all their faces.

CHAPTER TEN

Stark

The look on this artist's face makes my stomach sour. You'd think I was presenting him with an award or an elaborate gift. Maybe surprising him with a new car or something.

Not a box of Noland Elsinger's leathered human skin.

The only reason I took on this delivery task is because the other worker who was offered kept shying away. He didn't want to say why he didn't want to do it, but I know why. I overheard him talking with others. He's concerned he hasn't seen a drop of his money. He doesn't know that any of his work will actually pay off. He wants to question it, ask when and if they'll ever see it.

He wants out, but he'd never say it. He's too afraid.

So I sucked up my own disgust and offered to be the sole deliverer.

The artist in front of me takes the box from my grasp and opens it up, examining the pieces with his eyes and his fingers, petting each one like a furry animal. Skin from a hand is like a hamster. Pieces of face like tiny mice. And a chunk of carefully cut arm is like a rabbit.

All are pieces he's carefully handling as if they would squeal if he held them too tight.

I tell the acid in my stomach to stay there. If I let it all out all over the supplies I'm giving this man, then he won't be able to use it. And I'll end up as a pile of ashes in the quad, too.

I'm convinced that's exactly what's happened to the No Name The Dignitary called out in the slaughter room. He hasn't shown up since that day. And the only thing that's shown up in his place was the ashes

I tossed on the field. I'm willing to bet if I was able to count the number of ash piles on those pedestals, it would match up to the amount of No Names who have gone missing since the few days I've been here.

So, instead, I smile at this man as I watch him examine each piece, no doubt planning how to utilize them into something worthy of The Dignitary's praise. An awkward belt. A pair of chaps. A decorative canvas that can be framed later. Hope tells me this man will gladly take the box soon so I don't have to think about holding these pieces of the professor for too much longer.

"Fine specimen you have here," he tells me. "I've never thought to use such materials. Sure, cow leather maybe. Or stretched canvas at times. Tons of fabrics. But this?" He holds up a tiny finger-sized piece. "This is just outstanding. The exact reason why I was called here. There's no finding material like this on the shelf of any supply store."

He dangles the tiny piece between two fingers and sniffs it. My jaw clenches, hoping to bite back any rising bile.

"Do you have any idea what it's like? To hold something so powerful? It speaks to you, man."

Nodding my head is the only response I can bear to give.

"It's powerfully inviting. It's like it's giving me actual direction. It's my actual muse, begging me to put something together that will speak to the world."

I do my best not to exhale my relief when he takes the box from me. He even gives it a hug. I've seen children less thankful for Christmas gifts, even ones they had asked for for months.

"Is there anything else I can do for you?"

Today's job requires me to ask, and I hope he says no. I hope he tells me that he has everything that he could possibly need right in that box so I don't have to look at any more body parts today. I want to be done with this part.

He considers the offer, biting his lip and rocking his new toys in his cradled arms. "Actually, yes, there is."

Fantastic. Shit. My stomach ties itself into a knot. "What else do you need?"

"Oh, just a little advice is all." The gleam in his eyes is terrifying. "I have the pleasure of adding a piece blindly to the already accumulated finished art. I know that the most well-thought-out pieces are the ones that will make the most impact. And there's just so much I can do. The options are limitless! But since I'm going at it blindly, I don't know which object to choose."

"You're adding… blindly?" The memory of getting into this place to begin with flashes past my eyes. The folded paper where each man blindly added a piece of the drawing without knowing what was last added.

A majestic corpse. A silly game I used to play in art camp. A kids game to see what different art styles would create if they were applied to different areas to the same design. Blindly.

Holding a box full of corpse flesh, the title of the game has taken on a whole new meaning.

The look this man is giving those pieces takes it all a little further, too.

"I - I," I start to say. "I can offer my best."

"Perfect." He opens the box again to take in the supplies inside, then slams down the lid. "So my top two choices are leather boots or a book cover."

It's hard not to choke on the actual consideration of the two. How can I even offer a suggestion? Both are horrendous.

But I can tell I'm taking far too long without offering up anything. His eyes are questioning the reason for my pause.

I clear my throat. "These are both, um, fantastic choices. And of course you're the real artist here. So my opinion is only worth its weight in words."

He nods an agreement, but I can tell he still wants an answer.

So I take it seriously. If I found myself in such an unfortunate situation as to be like the man in the box — or what's left of him — what would I prefer to be crafted into for the rest of eternity? What would I want people to see me memorialized as?

A pair of boots would leave me at the bottom of some poor person's feet, constantly stepped on and kicked around. I'd get worn out, holes in my skin, then tossed away as if I never existed in the first place. That sounds awful.

On the other hand, a book cover would be held and loved on. It would hold the pages of a complete story. With relationships and growth and happy endings. It would protect that story, over and over. So that several people could enjoy it, love it, and revisit as often as they'd like. My skin, as horrible as it sounds, would provide so much more value and purpose.

"A book cover," I nearly vomit out. My souring stomach doesn't want to consider it any more.

He sucks in his cheeks to think about it. "A book cover, huh?"

Again, I nod. Yes, that's what I said. Now I'd like for some signal to leave this conversation for good. I have other things on my to-do list that have nothing to do with helping out cult members who think they're going somewhere better through an ascension via dead body parts.

"Great. Leather boots it is."

What? Why?

"You can leave now."

I take my signal and go, doing my best not to slam the door behind me. Clearly the man I just talked to, behind door number two, wasn't asking because he respected my opinion. He was asking because he wanted to know what *not* to create using what I just gave him.

Of course that's why he asked. I don't know why I thought maybe he respected my opinion. I know I'm the lowest man on the totem pole, just ready to be run over and shut down every step of the way.

The truth is, there's one for each of them. Ten people are sacrificed for The Circle. And each body is given to a specific member. They've been pre-picked and predetermined, coded by the numbers on their rooms. And this guy I just met got that professor. As horrible as Professor Noland Elsinger was, I'm not sure turning him into a spectacle of leather boots is what he deserved. But then I think about how he killed the girls in Volga and kidnapped Mills. I think about how he must have held her hostage and did only God knows what with her.

Maybe leather boots are better than he should get. Maybe he deserves to be trampled on and worn down until even his skin doesn't exist any more.

I make my way down the hall, passing doors numbered three through six. Before long, they'll each have a future box waiting for them. My fear is that Mills's name will be attached to one of those boxes before I can find her. When I reach door number seven, I realize it's wide open. I don't mean to look inside, but I do. What stares back at me is an above-average creepy smile. It's as if its overzealousness was waiting for me.

"Exciting, isn't it?" this man-child says. "I know we're supposed to be patient and wait our turn, but I just can't help myself. Every day, I'm waiting for the next door to get their gifts, counting down to when mine arrives."

"And when will yours arrive?" I have a feeling I know the answer. I did just deliver to two others. There are only five more doors to get there. But I want to be sure.

He claps his hands together in glee. "Five days!"

Exactly as I thought.

He lets out a little squeal. "Then I have three whole days to finish up before the rest of our lives!"

Less than a week, and depending on where Mills falls into the plan, possibly less.

I wish him luck—because what else could I do without drawing attention to myself?—and move on my way. Two doors greet me at the end of the hall. One opens to the other half of the floor, where Mills may be. The other offers stairs. I'm supposed to go downstairs, back to the room where No Names wait for the next task given to them.

But I should have time. Enough to take a peek. See if my assumption is right.

So, I scan the keycard I was given and open the door with a hiss. Everything on this half of the floor mirrors the half I just left. There are only a few minor differences, things most people wouldn't notice. But sometimes the loudest things are said in the minor details.

The numbers on the doors aren't as polished. The carpet on the floor is a little more worn. Parts of the walls are scuffed and scratched, just enough to say those who stay on this half of the floor aren't held in nearly as high regard as the half I just left. They're not as worthy.

Not worthy enough to stay alive long enough to kill themselves for their beliefs. It's a messed up mentality.

I pass rooms one and two. The doors are closed, but I already know they're empty. I just spent my time bringing pieces of this Number Two to the other Number Two.

Three is also closed, but I can hear movement behind the door. I put my hand against the door. I want to open it, peek inside, but I'm not called for here. Door four is open, though, and I can hear voices from inside.

With careful movements, I steal a glance. Just one, so I'm not caught. Inside are two women. One is a strawberry-redhead sitting at a table.

She's quiet, but she's whisper-calling out the names of colors. "Canary yellow, azure blue, grasshopper green."

There are a few glass clinks and then a voice that stops my heart from taking its next beat. "I have steel grey and black crow as well." The blonde holds up two jars and turns. I only catch a glimpse before I force myself to turn away. I don't want her to catch me staring. If she did, I wouldn't have a choice. I'd grab hold of her and whisk her away. I'd run out of here without a second thought. I'd make all the ruckus a single person could.

But there are too many eyes on me in this place. And if we both get caught, then we both end up cremated and scattered. Or worse.

And my heart can't handle that. She doesn't deserve that.

If Mills is in number four, then I only have two days to save her.

CHAPTER ELEVEN

Mills

"Can you hand me the red, please?" I open one palm out in the air and let the other guide the brush stroke I'm already on.

"You mean crimson?" Paula almost laughs out. Her voice is a happy whisper.

I'm so glad we came up with this idea. There's nothing like leadership on something that matters in the world of art and creativity. And better yet, we're doing the thing I always thought I was pretty damn good at. You could throw clay or paper mâché or fabric at me all day. None of it is going to compare to what I can do with a blank canvas.

If I'm going to save anyone in this world with art, it's going to be through painting.

Not to toot my own horn or anything, but what I've started to create here is already damn good. Taking one look at my part of the mural, the face of a lady painting her own face with a paintbrush, this was what I'm meant to do. Always have. I'm not so hesitant to even say I could be the Frida Kahlo of the Volga community. Toot. Toot.

"Here you go." Paula places the jar of red in my hand. I accept it and its place in the painting.

Her work is pretty kickass, too. Flowers. I know, I know. That sounds boring. But they're not. They're intricately detailed. Her rose petals are accentuated with droplets of dew. Tulip ripples look like I could actually feel their movement. And I don't know what the heck the other flowers are called, but their petals floof up like a pillow. I swear I could actually hold one in my hand and fluff my own face with it.

The only thing that hasn't been done yet is the space between my painting and hers, but we'll come up with something to merge the two, so they can become one. Something symbolic of the merging of two artists. A link of sorts, that flows from one half to the other of the retaining wall. It'll show everyone, including every No Name in this place, that any two people of this world can collaborate for the greater good. We can bridge the gaps, connect the details, create something that will no doubt move every heart whose eyes lay upon our mural today.

They'll get it. Their stupid jaws will drop and they'll get it.

It won't be long before *the* day happens, and the rest of the world might see it, too.

I mean, if Dali da Monet told The Dignitary the only way to save the world is through art, then this needs to be part of it: the mural that was driven by the desire to move others for the sake of art moving them.

I unscrew the crimson lid and dip my brush into it. A few strokes, and the painted lady's lips are painted, too. Fresh. Clean. Bright. Completely and perfectly in line with the lines of her face and the soft strokes of her hair. My painted lady feels like a beautiful spirit, someone who will watch over the commune with full heart and extra care. She'd guide the hearts of every viewer to find it within themselves to love their own craft.

"You're doing a great job, Mills," Paula tells me as she makes her finishing touches on a pointed leaf. "You've really found your niche."

Correction, I found my way back to it. If and when The Dignitary gives me another craft, I'll politely decline and ask where I can put my true skills to work.

After all, you can't perfect every craft, or nothing actually becomes perfect. Focusing on one that actually makes sense to you is the only way to become a master of anything.

"What do you think you're doing?" A third voice joins us. It's the same No Name that knocked on our door before. The same one that judged my poor little butterfly before it ever had a chance to be loved by anyone else's eyes.

I take one more look at my work and stand up. My hand rests on the top of the retaining wall. I contemplate hopping on top of it, but that might come across a little too cocky, which probably won't go over well at all. It doesn't stop me from showing off the pride I have over what we've already done. "We're painting." I could have thrown "duh" in there for good measure, but at least I held that back.

"This wasn't an assignment." I don't know what this No Name's problem is. Seriously, they always pop in and out with minimal conversation. I always assumed they just did as they were told and ignored the rest. I didn't realize they were some kind of art police.

"No, it's not, but our hearts told us it was necessary." It's the truth. Not like I had any reason to lie about it. And hell if I was going to stop myself from doing the one thing that always pulled me in, especially if it'll help save the world, including the sour -ooking man in front of me.

Doesn't he get it? Isn't he here for the same purpose?

Well, not the exact same. But he should still understand, right? And support? Isn't that his job?

"Unacceptable." He takes a step forward and crosses his arms.

Another No Name sees the soon-to-be-altercation and decides he's also a part of the irrelevant art police. He stands next to the first one and crosses his arms, too. It's like these two think they're bouncers at Club Fun and we apparently did something that prevents us from getting in any further.

I swallow back my fear. There's no time like the present, when I've found my confidence again, to question what's right in front of me. "I'm sorry, this is unacceptable to who? The Dignitary? Or *you*? Because from where I'm standing, your opinion doesn't trump hers, and it never will. I suppose that's why you're a No Name, and not one of the chosen artists, isn't it? It's not like *you* have a say in who does what or why or how."

Instantly, I regret it. I know I'm right. This guy doesn't have what it takes to appreciate a work of art when he sees it. There's zero chance he actually knows how to create anything himself. But he, and all the other No Names, work on a false sense of power. There's bound to be one or two who let it go to their heads. Clearly the two in front of us have let that happen already.

"You don't know what you're saying," the first one says.

"You have no idea how much trouble you've gotten yourself into," the second one chimes in.

It takes me two seconds to realize what's happening as they both uncross their arms, speed toward us, and pin our backs against the retaining wall. Wet paint feels sticky through my clothes and my arms desperately try to fight off the first man's grip.

Within milliseconds, both of these jokers have us restrained, holding our wrists in vise-like holds, directing us away from our mural. I have no idea where they're taking us, but I have a feeling it's not to have tea with The Dignitary. That ship has come and gone. The No Name police have decided to take matters into their own hands.

CHAPTER TWELVE

Livvy

"Livvy, I didn't want to say it because it makes me sound like a complete ditz. But this thing is *so* cute!" Mariëtte pats our new bunny on the head, and I watch its ears press back in delight.

She reminds me a lot of Harriet, the perfect shade of grey and the twitchy pink nose. But she has a little white spot right above her tail that denotes her as a completely different bunny. She's going to need a good name. Something that gives her a strong identity. Something we can call her that she would recognize. That's step one in making a connection. And if she's going to do what I need her to do, we're going to need to connect right away.

"I was thinking, we should name her Snuffles," Mariëtte's ditz-voice breaks into my thoughts.

I'm sure my face probably gave away what I felt about that name. Snuffles? That's the name of some pet that doesn't do anything but sleep and poop. Or the name of a kid's stuffed animal that gets tossed in the trash bin three weeks after playing with it. That's not a strong name for a trained rabbit. Especially not one that is going to aid me in saving my brother and best friend.

Mariëtte laughs. "Ok, so you don't like Snuffles. You've got a better idea?"

I don't even hesitate, "Bridget. She just kinda looks like a Bridget, you know?" It's my turn to give her a pat. She gives me a twitchy nose-kiss back. I think she likes the name.

Mariëtte gives another giggle. "You definitely seem to know better than me. I think she likes it."

"I think she does, too."

We spend a few minutes petting Bridget and feeding her little nibbles of hay. She's taken to us pretty well so far, but I know how animals can be in their new homes: unsure and untrusting. I want her to know we're her people. I want her to see us as both fun and safe. It doesn't take much time before she bounces between our laps, eagerly waiting for the next snack of hay we pull out for her. Already, she's learning what to expect if she goes to either of us. A little bit of food is all that it takes. Training Bridget is going to be a breeze.

"So what do we do with her first? How exactly are we supposed to test her oxytocin levels?"

I pull out another pinch of hay and watch Bridget bounce back over to me. "I think the best way for us to log it is to watch her behavior." Bridget nibbles her snack out of my hand, then moves her body in a circle to face Mariëtte again. Before Mariëtte can even reach for another bit of hay, Bridget is in her lap, nuzzling her.

"You see how she nearly ran over to you? When oxytocin levels go up, she'll get excited. She knows you have food, and she's going to do whatever it is she thinks you want her to do in order to get that food."

Mariëtte pulls out another bit of hay and feeds it to her. "She definitely knows how to get a little snack. That's for sure."

"Wait right here." I move myself off the floor and go to my brother's pantry. Since Stark has decided to infiltrate a cult, I decided his apartment is now mine. At least for the time being. Someone has to make sure the place doesn't burn down.

I know he doesn't have anything in the fridge, but I also know he's the kind of guy to buy every snack he can and stuff his pantry shelves with it. Cereal, granola bars, crackers, some weird cheese in a can I dare not touch and… bingo. Dried fruit mix. I tear open the top and reach in for a small handful of dried strawberry slices, banana chips, and blueberries.

Clutching my new stash in my hand, I bring it over to Mariëtte and Bridget and sit down across from them. "I'm curious. What do you think she'll do if I hold out a different treat?"

"I mean, a handful of dried fruit definitely looks better to me than that other stuff."

"Sure, but let's see." I pull out a blueberry. It's shriveled up and dry, but I'm sure it's still a lot sweeter than the hay, and it was Harriet's favorite treat. It rolls slightly in the center of my palm, and I call her over. "Bridget, come see what I have." When she doesn't turn around to me, I try something else. I give her a little whistle. "Wheet-woo." It works. I get her attention.

Our little bunny twitches her nose. I hold up the blueberry to show her what I have. She knows I have something different than what we've been feeding her. But she doesn't trust it yet. She gives one little hop in my direction and pauses, twitching her nose some more. A second hop makes her seem a little more interested. If a rabbit could crawl, that's what she's doing. Tentative steps to see what I'm offering her and if it'll feel as good to eat as the hay did.

"Well, that's definitely not an excited bunny," Mariëtte decides.

"Nope. She's not excited. Which means her oxytocin levels are-"

"Definitely lower than before."

"Exactly, but let's see if she eats it and what happens after that."

It takes a few minutes for Bridget to get close enough to do a thorough inspection of my offering. She sniffs at it, bounces a little back and forth, and nudges my hand. But she doesn't take it. Unlike Harriet, this bunny is not interested in blueberries.

I can't help but frown.

"Well, I think it's safe to say that Bridget's oxytocin levels are not triggered by dried blueberries."

"I guess not."

"But didn't you say that we're going to train her, too?"

I nod and sigh. I know I was being hopeful for a quick turnaround, but it sure would have been nice to have someone on my side. I'd feel like I could actually help out both Stark and Mills.

"Yeah. If we can find a treat she likes, then we can get her to do other tricks. The more the treat spikes her oxytocin, the happier she is with it. The happier she is with the treat, the easier it'll be to get her to do different things to reward her with it."

Mariëtte thinks about this for a moment. "Livvy, can I be honest with you?"

That's a weird question. I don't know if I've ever given her reason to think she couldn't be honest with me. I give her the go-ahead with a nod.

"Olivia, I get the feeling that this rabbit isn't about our grade or the workshop it's for. All this talk about oxytocin levels seems… I don't know. It seems juvenile for you? It's like you're stretching for something that might fit the assignment without it actually being for the assignment. You know what I mean?" When I don't give her an answer, she cocks an eyebrow at me and says, "I get the feeling that you're using this rabbit for something else."

There it is. Point blank. She's called me out.

I still don't respond, but she's definitely right. I guess I haven't been completely honest with her.

"Don't get me wrong. This is a lot more fun than taking blood samples from a sorority sister. And I'm pretty sure as long as we word it well enough, we'll pass with flying colors. But there's definitely something else up your sleeve, Olivia Landon." She clears her throat, then says, "Can I try one? Maybe a strawberry?"

I pinch one of the dried strawberries out of my palm and hand it to her, curious where she's going with it.

She holds it out in her palm on her lap just like I did with the blueberry and calls Bridget over with a little click of her tongue. Bridget starts the same dance she did with me. One tentative hop, pause, a second tentative hop. A longer pause.

"The thing is, you don't have to tell me whatever it is. I get secrets, trust me. We all need to keep a few to ourselves once in a while. If you don't feel like you want to tell me why training a rabbit is important to you right now, then don't. It's okay. I don't need to know why. If it's important to you, then it's important to me and we'll make it happen."

Bridget twitches her nose, and I watch her ears do a little wiggle.

"But I do need you to know this. I look out for my girls, and not just the ones who share the same Greek letters on their shirts. It's all the girls around me, especially the ones who look after one another. All it takes is one look while you're talking about this rabbit and I know. There's something bigger than a pet bunny here."

Bridget tilts her head a little, aiming her nose in the air.

"We don't know each other all that much, but I know that look. And I know you miss your friend. Mills, right? And I know your brother didn't go on a random vacation just to leave you to take care of his apartment. The way you walk through his place makes it seem like you're hopeful he's going to walk through the door any moment."

Bridget nudges at Mariëtte's hand, and she brings her palm forward so the bunny can get a closer look.

"So if you don't want to tell me what's going on, that's a-ok by me. I sorta left out of that picture when I got the impression that you were going to take care of… whatever is actually going on. But I'm still going to be here, by your side. And if it's going to take working with a rabbit to jump through hoops of fire or whatever, then I'm going to stick with it. I'll do what I can to get this rabbit's oxytocin levels up high enough to crawl through a tunnel or jump through fire or do backflips. Whatever you need."

Bridget perks her ears up and snags the strawberry out of Mariëtte's hand. Her little fluff of a tail bobs back and forth in excitement.

Mariëtte smiles at me. "Guess our Bridget likes strawberries more than she likes blueberries."

I nod, and think about what Mariëtte said. I close my eyes and make the decision to let her in. Girls stick together, right? And if I'm going to stick with Mills, I might as well have Mariëtte on my team, too.

"Stark infiltrated a cult that's holding Mills hostage, and I need a rabbit to help me get them out of there."

Her eyebrows arch. She probably doesn't believe a single word. I know, it all sounds crazy to me, too.

I bite my lip, thinking about how to continue. "I don't even know if it'll work, but I have to try something. I need to get hold of him, a-la carrier pigeon style. Except, we don't have a pigeon. We have a rabbit. A Harriet. And I believe she can at least help me figure out how to get them out."

"Well, I guess there's more riding on this rabbit than I thought." She leans over and steals another strawberry piece out of my hand. "Looks like we've got a bit more training to do. Let's teach this rabbit to bust them out of there."

CHAPTER THIRTEEN

The Dignitary

Who would have thought something as simple as a broadcast would be so complicated? I didn't think it would take thirty odd people to do all the things it takes to make something like this work. Shouldn't it just be pressing a button to make it happen? I hate the technical things in life. It's why I never did well with science and math. But, hey, that's why I have these men doing all the work for me. I don't have to think about every detail to make it all work. I just have to overhead it to make sure it happens. And happens well. Dali da Monet is counting on me to do so.

So these so-called workers better make sure it happens.

The amount of computer screens in one room is overwhelming. Placing an order for them was frustrating. I had to take whatever money was saved up to get them all here. It's worth it, though. It's not like any of these people actually need money. Not where they're going. It seems like everywhere I turn, there's yet another view on another screen, all pointing to the courtyard where our display is being pieced together, until the final display will take form.

The final display. When the Supermoon reveals itself in the sky, and the light from it lights up the whole place to open up the portal into ascension. At least for me and the selected chosen ones.

The rest will get their turn, eventually. They'll drink their tea and fall wherever the fates land them. And those who feel they need to reserve? There will always be another Supermoon. And I'm sure there will always be someone willing to call in a higher power using their bodily vessel. All it takes is for me to find the right person to take the wheel after.

But who?

Maybe it'll be ten true ascensions after all. Maybe one of those extra-special recruits will be willing to stay behind. Do my bidding for me.

No; for Dali da Monet.

For the world. For all of us. Maybe I'll find someone who can take over and take control, continue on the plans of the elders, our collective ancestors, to keep the love and knowledge of Earth alive.

Until the next Supermoon comes to take them. Or perhaps another sign from the stars. Who knows. Not I. My human form knows nothing.

I will only know *all* when I can crawl into my highest self, using the collective power to guide my subconscious into the truths and knowledge.

There is only one face I have in mind who might be able to take my place. Once I'm done observing this tech room I'd rather not be in, I'll ask if he's ready to train, to call on the voice of Dali da Monet and learn how to hone in on it for the others. Based on his eagerness, I'm sure he will gladly be appointed as the next Dignitary and keep the beauty going.

I sure hope so.

If not, it'll be this group of chosen artists and that's it. We'll be saved, but the rest of the world will be screwed.

Looking over one No Name's shoulder, I notice the screen in front of him is focused on the ground. "Why is there a camera aimed here?" I ask.

It shouldn't be aimed at the feet of everything. That does absolutely nothing. Our art should be on full display, so everyone can witness the truth of beauty and art and hear the message of all of us: The end is coming for all of us. In time, she will take every last one of us. And we have a choice. We can honor the beauty in art, or we can passively ignore it and be doomed.

The No Name turns around in his chair. "Ma'am, you told us to have cameras at every angle. I figured this would include one of *every* angle." I take his literal tone into consideration. These men do me so well. They take my words seriously. It's too bad their ascension hasn't come yet. It may not ever.

That's okay. They're doing their duty right here on Earth's plane. Without their support, there would be no spreading of any message. There would be no connection. There would be no perfect ascension for me and the others. There would be no worldwide broadcasting because there's nothing that would help me understand how any of this system works. I'm thankful I can tell them what I need and, as long as they don't screw up, they'll make it happen.

I think we can all agree that when people screw up, they become useless.

"I see," I tell him.

The sweat beading on his brow tells me that he's unsure of what to expect next. He's trying to judge my reaction, to see if I think he's one of the screw-ups or not.

He's not. Not yet.

"Good job." I pat him on the back and can feel his instant relief.

Moving onto the next desk, I look at the screen behind the No Name sitting. "And you. What genius have you put together for our event?" According to the screen, it doesn't look like much. Just a plain view from the left side. Right where fold-out seats will be, for guests to bear witness to the final event.

"We have everything covered at this angle, ma'am. We had a fuzzy image earlier, but have cleared it up since and we're all ready to go."

"Make sure you keep it that way." Fuzzy images will never work. Who can observe any of the fine details with a fuzzy image?

Again, I move onto the next. This No Name has a screen, too. But it doesn't show anything outside. It's full of senseless numbers and words that drabble on like incoherent thoughts. It better be something good. "And you? Tell me you've got whatever this is," I wave my hand at the screen, "under control."

This man sighs. That's my first clue that something isn't right. Something is wrong. It's not perfectly-perfect.

"So, we have a private server I can code to stream everything on the day of. March fifteenth. The problem is, I don't know if the VPN and TOR browser will actually reroute everything to keep anyone from tracking where it came from. It might not be as anonymous as we were hoping for. "

I swallow the hot anger collecting in my throat. "Are you saying it's not working?"

"No, ma'am. I'm just - just - just unsure if it's going to work the way we want it to or if there will be a leak of information somewhere. I need a little more time to do some testing. To make sure it is working the way we want without any gaps."

"Testing?" I do my best not to bark out the word. "You should be thankful. Up until this task, you have had it easy. Small jobs that just whittle the time away. You could have been spending some of that time learning how to make this part happen. You could have been saving up your time and energy so that there would *be* no gaps later."

The way he shakes his head at me is all I need to claim this as the next red flag. He has screwed up. He didn't use his time wisely. He rushed and wasted and now we're stuck with something that may not even work.

"You," I tell him. "You need to leave."

"But," he tries to fight back.

One meaningful look from me and he stops in his own tracks. He understands, gets up, and he leaves the tech room. Right where two other No Names will escort him out. He accepted his fate the moment it was given to him. Looking around the room, most of the other men have accepted where his fate is taking him, too.

It's okay, though. He'll become part of the show in his own way. His ashes will do better work than he has shown anyway.

"Ma'am?" another No Name calls out, and I brush off my irritation. What does this one have to offer? Could he be a beacon of light I need? We need?

"Ma'am? After hearing what he said, I have a suggestion if you'd like to hear it."

I consider this for a minute. On one hand, a lowly suggestion from someone who doesn't even need a name couldn't possibly make a difference. On the other hand, this is someone who saw a problem and is offering a possible solution. A solution to this technical problem that's completely Greek to me.

Dali da Monet needs a solution.

We all do.

This can't go wrong. I can't have any more flubs. The world needs to hear our message and The Circle needs to ascend. I need to! It's my duty to make sure these souls will be saved, and I can't. Have. Anything. Go. Wrong.

Intrigued, I tell him, "Go on."

"Well, ma'am. Sometimes with these things, you need to test them in a real-life scenario. Put them through the same steps you would in a live feed. That way, you can figure out which pieces are wrong so you can fix them. It gives the most accurate reading so you can come up with the most accurate fix."

I ponder this scenario. So we'd place everything out in the open, all the paper mâché pieces and the clay sculptures sitting in the sacrificed dust. The completed pieces wouldn't be done yet, but that's okay. It's just a test, right? We'll make sure the final pieces connect after. That's where the real magic will happen. That can be saved for the ascension date itself. It'll be a sampling, and that might be enough. Enough for a scenario close enough to the real thing.

"Can we do that?" I ask? "Can we test it out safely, or will this…system thing give everything away?"

He clears his throat. "As of right now, the percentages are on our side. There's a slight chance it won't be as secure and anonymous as we'd like. But, if we run a test, it'll just be a regular viewing, right? None of the actual magic will happen. It'll be like any other art show.

"We can invite some people from the public. People who have an interest in the arts without having the talent themselves. They might not view the entire show, but they don't know that. And we can air it on a locked server, tracking the anonymity if and when it goes wide. If it happens to slip and air publicly, it'll be an extra viewing for those who stumble across it. But no harm no foul, since it's not the real thing. Just practice. No one would know the difference."

No one except the people we invite.

Would that be okay?

I close my eyes and drop my head back as far as my neck will allow. When that starts to cramp up, I relax, move my body to the floor. When a few mumbles irritate me, a few of the No Names shush them. They understand. I need quiet. I'm not even sure if it'll work with the hums of the running computers, but I try anyway. I need to know if this will work. Not just technically, but spiritually.

The cold floor licks my skin and ripples throughout my arms. I let the feeling overtake me, taking deep breaths and focusing my mind on her. On him. On them. On the universe. I picture all the masters of art and ask for their guidance. I want to hear their voices and feel their pull. This isn't my decision to make. It's theirs. So, I listen.

I allow the computer hums to fill me with their rhythm. I'm no longer worried they'll distract because they become me, and I, them. The sounds seep into my blood, acting as a signal to call in the voices and guidances I'm after.

Ten minutes pass. Twenty. I stay in the same spot longer on the floor, calling to our artistic ancestors.

Sometimes it takes longer. I'm lucky because after an hour, I feel her voice.

Their voices.

They prickle in and out of me, from the tips of my toes all the way to my fingertips. They move up my arms and into my shoulders, pinching the back of my neck, too. Within seconds, the voices enter my mouth and coat my teeth, causing my saliva to thicken. Then, they push open my lips and allow the air to escape.

"Yes," they say.

And, yes, we will be holding a test run. A trial.

"Start making invitations. Be selective. Share them with the non-Memento Mori members who would *appreciate* an event such as this. And be quick. Everything needs to be selected, printed, and distributed in less than twenty-four hours. We need to get a move on it or we won't have enough time to test before the Supermoon arrives for us all."

Who knows, maybe we'll find new recruits for the next round after me. I'm sure my successor would be even more willing to take my place knowing he'll have names to utilize for himself.

CHAPTER FOURTEEN

Stark

I'm told she went against the rules. That she followed her instinct without being told how, creating something that wasn't ordered to be created. And now she and another girl are being punished.

My heart pounds against my chest, and I can feel my heated blood reach every organ inside. I know how horrible some of our jobs can be. And since one of mine was to deliver ashes to the scene of the show, I'm pretty sure it was someone else's job to make those ashes in a crematorium.

I haven't had time to come up with a plan. But since that's the case I need to come up with one quickly. If nothing else, I'll grab Mills and run like a rabbit. I'll take her as far as I can, run past every brainwashed meathead in this place. And if I get caught? I'll use anything I can get my hands on, including my hands themselves to beat them all away from her. Even if it means exhausting myself and taking the fall for it all. My chances against this many lackeys are slim, but I'll do whatever I need to do in order to keep her safe.

Standing in a room with one other No Name, I'm not sure what to expect. Things have moved quickly, and they move quicker every day. I even get the feeling that we've already been given more information than is necessary. Judging by the way The Dignitary talks, I get the feeling we were all supposed to know very little about everything. Every job was minute, every task minor. But now, we're given large tasks, complications that screw with my emotions and mentality. I suppose that's because word travels fast around the No Name crowd. The game of telephone gets played all too easily.

I'm sure it only took two rings of that proverbial telephone to get to The Dignitary so she could come up with a proper punishment. And now, it's up to me and this other nameless man to carry it out. So we wait. We wait until someone comes to deliver the message.

And while we wait, I consider the scenario over and over in my head.

They bring me Mills. I grab her. Knock however many people are around me out and run.

Fast. Hard. And without looking back.

"Exciting, isn't it?" the guy next to me asks.

At that moment, I decide his name is Ted. I don't like Ted very much and he definitely deserves a name that reflects that.

I don't respond. I just run the same words over and over in my head. Run. Hit. Run. Hit. Run. Run. Run.

"I mean, this job definitely pays more than the others. I can only imagine what my account is going to look like when this is all over."

Hit. Run. Run. Run.

"Which is, when you do that thing? After the Supermoon, right? It shows up, lights up the sky, the show goes off? And then what?"

Run. Run. Run.

"Then The Dignitary and the others get to do their thing. They'll be accepted into whatever realm they're going to and we'll all be millionaires, right?"

Millionaires? Is Ted for real? Does he really think anyone is paying him anything? Scratch that thought. It doesn't matter. Run. Run. Run.

"I know they've said after the show, it'll all be done, but I don't really want it to be over. I've never had exciting jobs before. And definitely nothing that pays with room and board as well. This is a good gig if you ask me."

Oh how I wish I could hit Ted right now. Right where it counts. But Mills will be through the door at any moment and I need to be ready.

"No retail gig can compare to the interesting things we get to see, too. The most I got from the shop was someone leaving a dookie in a changing room. That's just dirty. It never gave me the tingly feeling I get here. It's pretty damn perfect."

Exhale. Hit. Hit. Hit. Run.

The door opens. Here she comes. I'm getting ready. I'm…

There's a girl standing in front of us, escorted by two large No Names I don't want to name right now. But it's not Mills. It's a strawberry-redhead.

My heart sinks. All the adrenaline that had been building up instantly evaporates as if it never existed. I was so sure Mills would be delivered right here, and now I have a stranger staring back at me instead.

I wish I knew her real name. I have a feeling she deserves that much.

The No Name restraining her wrists with his hands speaks up. "One of you has the job to take her hands from me. The other," he looks at Ted, "has the job to guide her into solitary confinement. It's on the opposite side of the show area, behind the retaining wall a ways. You may need to walk a few paces further out to actually find it, but it's there, a row of single-seated, untouching buildings. She belongs in the first one you reach. It's the job of the walker to also lock the door behind him. Should you fail-"

Mentally, I say the same phrase he says out loud, "You will be punished. Severely."

The two men hand her over, and I can't help but to notice how she's walking. Her head is hanging so low, I can't even see her face behind a curtain of red hair. Her posture is slumped and her steps are sluggish. She's defeated. She accepted her fate the moment it was read to her.

But at least it's solitary confinement. Which means somewhere else, Mills is being delivered to two other No Names to another predetermined single-seated building.

What a choice of words for a single cell.

But at least she's not being taken to an incinerator. I'll take that as a loose win. A little bit of time has been added to my side again.

Choking back my distaste, I take the girl's hands from the man restraining her. But I don't hold tight. The man before me may have left red fingerprints on her skin, but I refuse to add to them. My grip isn't enough to keep her from escaping if she wanted. And as much as I fear what might happen to the both of us if she does, I don't believe she deserves to be hurt anymore than she already has. I wish she'd run.

A piece of me is surprised she doesn't bolt when I slightly nudge her to the direction of the door. In silence, we follow Ted out.

Once we get outside, I'm surprised to see no one is out here as well. I guess The Dignitary has everyone doing busy work tasks. Probably something dealing with the show while the artists work diligently in their rooms.

I think about how many people have red wristbands, the side Mills was on, the side that wasn't chosen.

Or should I say, how many people are left on the red side.

It's not many. And if they're going in order, Mills might be next.

There goes my hot blood pumping through my system again.

The courtyard isn't as far as I remembered last. I can still see the pile of ashes I helped deliver. And there are a couple new ones as well. Other No Names who strayed from their post. Or the bones of those who weren't chosen.

We all know where everything else on their bodies go.

Run. Hit. Run. That's still the plan, right?

The solitary confinement cells—let's face it, they're not rooms—are definitely further than I thought. That man was right; you can't see them standing in the courtyard itself. They're much further down and out of sight. We even have to weave through a few pine trees to get there. No one would know they're here if they weren't told.

Which means it'll also be easy to forget that anyone shoved off to the side were ever here to begin with.

This time, when I swallow, my spit tastes like acid.

Ted is in front of me a few eager paces, so I do the only thing I can think of. I whisper to the girl I'm holding. "What's your name?"

She perks up, lifts her head. I can see the tip of her nose peeking through her hair now. Just enough of a face to know it's there. "Paula," she whispers back.

It's good to know a real name exists here. If only she would run away.

"Paula, listen. I'm not going to fight you. If you want to make a run for it before we get there, I understand. I won't hold you back. I won't even mention anything about it. I'll even take the fall. Please, go. Leave this place. I wish I could help you more than this. I wish I could escort you out of this place myself, but I can't. I can't leave her behind." I try to rush my words so that Ted doesn't hear.

She stops in her tracks and I gulp again. Will she go? Save herself?

"I deserve whatever punishment The Dignitary sees fit." The conviction in her voice tells me even though the idea of solitary confinement is terrifying, her promise to the cult's warped belief system is even stronger. She's not going to run. I could let go of her completely and she would still willingly walk toward her punishment. With that, she continues her steps.

"But you were just painting. The exact thing that got you here in the first place, the thing that made all of these people want you here and praise you for. Why should you be shoved off to the side when you were only doing the thing they loved about you?" My whispers rush out. We're getting closer to our destination. I fear I don't even have the time to hear a response.

But she does respond. Right when Ted opens the door to toss her inside. He removes my loose grip with his hands and pushes her in. She raises her head, and for the first time, I see her full face past her hair. She's pretty. And young. Probably even younger than Mills. She has so much ahead of her, if she just walked away when given the chance.

"Who are you?" she asks.

That's when I realize I've said too much to her. She knows I'm not one of them.

The door closes. Ted locks it. He lets out a chuckle to me.

"Who are you? Did you hear that? Doesn't she realize where she is? Our identities in the realm of so-called reality haven't mattered since the moment we got here. We are all one. We're all Memento Mori." He scoffs again. "Who are you? What a joke."

CHAPTER FIFTEEN

Livvy

"So, you're telling me that creepy place off Blackwell is a cult commune?" Mariëtte's words both sound giddy and in disbelief. "I'd say that's hard to believe, but based on all the other crap going on in Volga, I mean, that's just the icing on the cake. It makes total sense."

She shakes her head some more and whispers to herself, "A cult. Right here in Volga. And they say that Greeks are strange."

"You have to admit, some of the things you Greeks do are a little out there," I chime in. "But, yeah, this is for real. I saw it with my own eyes. They're all about artsy stuff. You should see this place, M. It's stale as anything. Everything is perfectly trimmed and proper. Not a single thing is out of place. It's as if it's one giant blank canvas. Everyone even wears the same damn thing."

Mariëtte squinches up her face. "Like hoods?"

Prickles run down my spine. "Thank goodness, no. Not quite the hood you're thinking. I don't know if I could stomach knowing my brother is in there if they were hooded with pitchforks and torches. It's more like they're wearing jumpsuits made of linen."

"Linen jumpsuits, huh?"

"Again, plain and sterile. As if they're waiting for paint and color to be added later."

Bridget the rabbit bounces over to us from her pen on the other side of the room. We let her out to explore, hoping she would show us if she remembered coming to our laps would earn her food.

She sniffs around the small dining table. I'm sure stray grains of rice or potato chip crumbs have been left behind from Stark. Sometimes rabbits can be just like dogs like that. They can sniff out the food left behind, scavenging for the tastiest pieces.

"And, oddly enough, Stark fit right in." I play the scene again in my head. All those men circled around us, passing around the same piece of paper, folding it in just the right way so no one could see what was added before the next person drew on it.

Majestic Corpse. That's what Stark had called it. What a morbid name for what's supposed to be a fun art game.

"Mariëtte, we've got to do something to get them out of there."

"So what exactly is your plan, Liv?" She leans in toward me, waiting to hear whatever plan I'm about to come up with on the spot. Because, clearly, I don't have a solid one thought out.

"About that. I've only gotten so far. Stark's in there now. He's going to find Mills. I need to be ready at any moment to bust them both out of there, but I need to know what's happening inside first. I can't exactly roll up in his car and wait indefinitely by the gate. It's not like they'll let me in to visit or anything. I have no doubt that even if it doesn't look like it, there are eyes and ears everywhere, waiting to give people like me a one-way escort out of there."

"I see." She taps her fingers on the carpet floor, trying to get Bridget's attention. But she's too busy searching another corner of the room, probably nibbling on something she's not supposed to.

"So you're planning on using a rabbit as what? Some kind of communicator?"

I shrug. It does seem a little half-ass, when she puts it that way. "I guess so."

"Livvy, it's genius, really!"

"Yeah?"

"Yeah! Think about it. If this works, we can send in any message we want without anyone knowing. Who would expect a cute little rabbit to be a top-secret spy to an infiltrator and the girl he loves?"

My cheeks run hot. "I didn't say he loves her." I can picture Mills slapping me on the shoulder for ever suggesting it. Though, I've always thought it pretty loudly.

"You didn't have to. Dude literally put himself in one of the most psychologically dangerous situations you can imagine simply to save her. That smells a lot like love to me."

We sit in a few quiet moments while Bridget makes a few hops to explore other areas of the apartment. Once in a while, she twitches her ears as if she's hoping we'd start talking again. It's like she is listening to us, waiting for her moment to join in and give her own two cents about the plan.

"Wheet-woo," I blurt out a whistle, and her ears perk up even more. She freezes in that position, curious about the sound and where it came from.

"Wheet-woo," I try again. This time, the curious bunny turns her entire body in my direction and makes a few slow hops toward me.

"Quick, hand me one of those strawberries." I hold out a hand toward Mariëtte.

She reaches over to the plate near her and picks up a slice of fresh strawberry. After the last time we spent training, we thought we'd try a juicer version of the fruit she actually liked. A little sweeter taste might give her a bigger incentive to do a bigger job.

You know, higher oxytocin and all that.

Mariëtte hands the piece to me, and I make the whistling noise again. "Wheet-woo."

When I can tell I have Bridget's attention, I hold out the strawberry. Her nose gives fast, tiny twitches in excitement. A few fast hops and she's in my palm, devouring the strawberry piece in as few nibbles as possible.

"Look at that," Mariëtte says. "Think she'll do it again?"

"Only one way to find out."

Mariëtte copies the same movement I did. She holds out a piece of strawberry and gives her best *wheet-woo* whistle. Bridget hears it, turns, and races to the strawberry.

Mariëtte and I both squeal in delight. She's doing it. She's really doing it.

I decide to test her a little more. I toss out another whistle, but I brush off Mariëtte's offer when she reaches to the strawberry slices.

Bridget looks confused at first. She's searching out an offering, probably wondering why she doesn't see it. I give out a second whistle, and she jumps toward me. A third and she hops excitedly, right into my lap.

"Good girl!" I give her praise and pets, and then I throw my hand out toward Mariëtte. She tosses me a piece of strawberry and I catch it. Instantly, Bridget finds it and accepts it happily.

Next step, we just need to figure out how to teach her to hold a piece of paper, follow a sound, drop it at Stark's feet, and find her way back. No problem. Easy peasy.

At least I know what I'm going to write in my first note. Exactly what Stark told me to do, and proof that I kept it in mind.

Remembered the rabbit hole.

CHAPTER SIXTEEN

Mills

I don't know how long it's been since I've been locked in this tiny room. My brain wants to say an hour. My stomach says longer. Though, it's not like it hasn't been starved before. The tiny grumble it's giving me now isn't that big of a deal. I now know it can hang tight for a few days and I'll still be fine.

Not that I want to be in here for a few days. Without anyone to talk to. Without any interaction. Without anything to paint or craft or create with at all.

My mind will get bored quickly. It'll drive me insane.

The man who man-handled me into this cell didn't exactly tiptoe his way here. It was like he was glad to toss me in like a caged dog. I can't decide if that means he's reveling in the little bit of power he has, or if what I did really was that out of line.

I wouldn't want to upset Iris. I don't know if I could handle disappointing her like that.

My feet pace back and forth. I've already counted it several times, memorizing the footsteps it takes to get to one side and the next.

Eleven. It takes eleven steps before I turn around and do it all over again.

When I'm done with that stroll, I turn around and do it again. Eleven steps turns into twenty-two. Then thirty-three. And again and again and again.

I count up to four hundred sixty three, then stop.

No one is coming for me. Not now. Not after what I did.

The only light that shines in is through the seams of the door and a little slit inside of it. It's not a lot. But with adjusted eyes, I can make out the outlines of everything in my *cozy* little room.

I flop down on the sorry excuse for a bed. It's literally a cardboard box with a ratty yarn blanket. The blanket smells like mold, and when I touch the edges, it feels wet. I'm not exactly excited to hold it, so I don't. It can stay on the other side of my box while I think about what I did like a punished little kid.

I gathered materials myself. I came up with the idea. I dragged Paula out of that room and marched over to the retaining wall. I put one brush in my hand and one in Paula's. I dipped the brushes into paint and I put that paint to the wall.

This is my fault. Not just my punishment, but Paula's, too.

Oh no. Paula. My stomach drops as far down as it can. It's my fault she's locked up in solitary confinement, too. She doesn't deserve that. She was a good girl. She did what she was told. She quietly stayed in her lane, head down, and was ready to rock and roll without question.

She did everything in the name of Dali da Monet from day one. She's the perfect Memento Mori member, and I screwed it up for her.

I. Screwed. It. Up. If it weren't for me, she would be back in her room, quiet and cozy under her covers, just waiting for the next assignment to no doubt nail down.

My hands fling to my face, and I let out the biggest frustrated scream my lungs can manage. My throat burns with the force as the sound bounces back at me. I have no idea what's in store for me, but I couldn't live with myself if Paula gets any residual punishment when she isn't responsible for the mistake at all.

A mistake. That's all it was. And now I have to pay for it with my time, hunger, and whatever energy is left in me.

I wonder if Paula can hear me. I lift myself off my box-bed and press my body against the locked door. "Paula!" I yell as loud as I can. "Paula! Can you hear me?"

I wait, hoping to hear a response. But the only thing I hear back is silence.

"Paula!" I hit the door with my fists. "Paula! I'm sorry!"

It's no use. She either doesn't hear me, or she won't respond.

My fist slams against the door again, and I can feel my entire body give away on itself. "I'm so sorry, Paula. So sorry." I slide down to the dirty floor. It's no wonder she isn't responding, that is if she can hear me at all. I don't blame her for being angry with me. I wouldn't want to talk to me, either.

I deserve this. Under Dali da Monet's grasp, I deserve this. I should have never dragged Paula into my shenanigans. I should have gone off on my own to test the limits of my abilities instead of dragging her into this mess.

My hand reaches the dirt covering the floor. I pick it back up and watch it leave a print in the mess. Again, I place it down and make another. The repetitive movement reminds me of Monet himself, blotches upon blotches from up close, who knows what when you step back.

I take in a deep breath, letting the air fill up my lungs. When I let it out, I can feel the way my heart beats faster, then slower, with the intention to calm me down.

I wonder if the collective voice would approve of this as art. Without any other materials, this is all I have to work with. I suppose I'll continue to make handprints in the dust until I hear her, they, it, whomever speak to me directly.

Then I'll know what to do.

That's how these things work, right?

"Paula!"

CHAPTER SEVENTEEN

Stark

A new day, a new room. If it weren't for the fact that I've been forced to get used to it in such a short time, I'd get dizzy. But here I am again, standing in a room full of No Names. Some faces I know well. Some, I've never met before. Which makes me wonder, how many of us are there? And where on earth do they all come from?

Is the world really so full of lonely people who will believe anything when given just enough praise and money to feel worthy?

I wish I could bust everyone out of here. Blow the whole place up and let every last person scatter into a safe corner of the world where they'll be loved and fed and given a comfortable place to live where they can be themselves. Truly themselves. Not some shell filled up with the ideals of some fiery red headed lunatic.

One of the No Names I don't recognize joins me where I stand. He's sipping on a goblet of water, like the King of England or something. The thought passes by me to slap it out of his hands and wake him up from this dream he thinks he's living in. But there are too many eyes and ears here. And if I slip up, who knows what will happen.

Not just to me, but to that poor girl, Paula. And Mills, too.

I make a mental note to visit solitary confinement later. I need to know which one Mills is in. And then I need to find a way to get her out of there. And out of here. Though, thinking about Paula's conviction to this place, there's a piece of me that wonders if Mills has fallen for the lies she's been told, too.

Oh. My. Heart. How will I get her out if she has?

"Are you on the tech team, too?" the water goblet guy says. I'll call him Arthur, as in King Arthur. And without letting me answer him, he continues. "It really is something, isn't it? The amount of work going into such a performance."

"Yeah," I tell him.

Though I haven't been a part of any tech team. If anything, I feel barely alive serving on a death team since the moment I've started here. But I've heard mumbles of a show. These Mori people, they're planning something big. And if I know anything about cults, I know their big ideals call for big devastation.

"I mean, I think I got lucky. I know nothin' about computers and gizmos. Put me in front of anything like that, and I'll end up deleting everything on it. Or breaking it somehow. I only get the simple things. Plug it in and hit start. Thank goodness my job is just to hang a couple of cameras here and there. There's not much to screw up except an angle."

"Yeah, you got the easy gig, that's for sure." This is a voice I remember. Bugs. The same cocky guy who thinks he has the world on a string. The way his words dangle in the air, I suppose he's also on the tech team. Judging by where he's had his hands before, that would mean he's dipped into a little bit of everything. "You should try testing the software some of these jokers are pulling together. There are bugs every which way." Bugs's forehead starts to glisten with sweat. "But I'm great with them. Log them quickly, get them fixed, and move on."

"Bugs?" I ask him. This time echoing his words, not the nickname I gave him. "What kind of bugs?"

He considers things for a moment, scratching at his chin and staring off into space. "Nothing big. A few fuzzy pictures that were cleared up. A broken login screen that took two minutes to fix. Nothing like what that one No Name came across."

Arthur stops in mid water-sip, bug eyed and still.

I'm afraid to ask, "What did he come across?"

The two of them glance at each other. They look around the room. When satisfied no one is watching them or purposefully listening in on our conversation, Bugs answers. "Something bad."

Okay, that wasn't exactly the detailed response I was hoping for.

"Bad," Arthur agrees.

And in the simple word, I understand. Whatever it was, it was bad. Bad enough not to talk about, bad enough for that No Name to disappear like the others. Bad, bad.

A few silent moments, and it's clear that these two aren't going to continue to give me any information unless I ask for it. But I don't want to prod in places that will make them clam up more. So, I bring up the thing that Arthur seemed confident with. "It must be pretty great working with the cameras, right? Setting them up in all the perfect spots?"

He nods enthusiastically. "Yup! It's fantastic! Just a few wires and adjustments and bing-bam-boom, done. And it pays well, too."

"That does sound great," I tell him. "Do you get paid for each camera?"

He looks at me, confused. "Each? No. My job is just one camera."

That sounds about right. The more work The Dignitary can hand out, the more purpose she can feed into each of her lemmings.

"Well, of course, but I bet it's the best looking camera out there."

He smiles and drinks again from his water goblet. "I know I've done Dali da Monet proud."

"The Dignitary, too!" Bugs exclaims.

"I'm sure you did." Maybe he can tell me where all the cameras are. Where they're pointed, where everyone's focus is going to be at the end of all days when the comet comes. "So where is yours?"

"Mine? Oh, it's the first one you can see, pointed at the leftmost pillar. It's mostly empty now. Just a weird looking paper mâché knife or something."

Paper machete. It's Mills's paper machete.

"But once the last pieces are done, I'm sure it'll be amazing. Maybe the best collage they all come up with," he finishes.

A collage, that's what they're putting together. A bunch of separate art pieces collected together for a singular message: Beautiful art is death. The perfect majestic corpse. The perfect memento mori. And they're going to film it.

I suck in a deep gulp of air, feeling the way my heart pumps blood into every extremity. "I have no doubt, your camera will catch the best images. Because the others…" I let it dangle.

"Well, they're on the other pedestals, obviously."

"I guess it'll give all the people who don't show up for trial a taste of everything, too."

This is news to me. A trial? A trial show? What does that mean? My face must show my confusion.

"Oh, you haven't heard yet, then?" Bugs chimes in. "We're putting everything to the test, to make sure it all goes without a hitch. The Dignitary doesn't want to be up for ascension facing some kind of problem. Dali da Monet only welcomes perfection, and if we don't make sure the set up is absolutely perfect, then it'll reflect on Her."

"And the rest of us," Arthur agrees.

"So they're actually inviting people outside the commune to come and see a preshow?"

Both of the men nod. But it's Bugs who clarifies. "Some of the No Names are putting together invitations now. We'll have about thirty seats, and not the entire collection set up yet. Those invitations are going to a very select crowd. The kind of people who appreciate eccentricities and creativity. The kind of people who might be in our position one day, or one even above us."

"If they're lucky enough, they'll be in the next Circle." Arthur finishes off his fancy glass of water and finds a coaster to leave it on.

A plan starts to form in my head. "And how are they selecting these audience members?"

Arthur shrugs. "I don't know. That's not part of my job. How about yours?" He looks to Bugs for clarification.

"Beats me. All I know is that they're getting the invitations ready at the factory now. They'll go out before tomorrow. I suppose it's someone else's job to come up with the list of names to send them to."

Or, if history has taught me anything, it's probably thirty people's jobs to come up with thirty names. And I'm not sure how to volunteer, but I'll be one of them. I know exactly whose name I'm putting on there, too.

The rabbit hole just got a little bigger.

CHAPTER EIGHTEEN

Livvy

"You sure this is going to work?" Mariëtte asks from the passenger's seat. She places her Joe's to-go cup of water into the cupholder and gives Bridget a little scratch behind her ears to reassure the rabbit on her lap.

We've only worked with Bridget for a day, yet every time, she followed our cues. As long as a strawberry is at stake, she will hop wherever we tell her. And she's gotten pretty good at holding a folded piece of paper in her mouth while taking directions, too.

But still, it's only been a day. It takes Stark longer to figure out a time to shave his five o'clock shadow. She's dropped several practice notes without going back for them. And half the time if she doesn't see a strawberry in sight, she gets distracted by something else and hops off track. So, no, I'm not sure this is going to work. Logic says we have less than a thirty percent chance. In fact, given that we're going somewhere this rabbit has never seen, with sounds she's never heard, and scents she's never smelled, we have a better chance of losing her altogether than for this to actually work.

"As sure as the sky is blue." But I'm not going to tell Mariëtte about my doubts. There's no reason to break her confidence in the process.

"And tell me again why we're not calling the police for help?" she asks with an uncertain tone.

I give her a little chuff. "Because you're a badass who knows how to fight as dirty as she needs to be. And I'm a Black girl who needs her brother and best friend out there now. Not next week or two when the police finally decide they have time on their schedule to dive into this mess."

She gives me a smile from the passenger seat. "Got it."

We drive a little longer, following the main roads to the dirt, down to the gravel road in front of the iron gate I'm now becoming so familiar with. I throw the car into park and hope no one behind that gate has seen or heard us roll up. Based on how I was greeted before with Stark, it's a safe bet that we'll be ignored. As long as we don't press the call button, we should be good.

One hit of that call button, and we'll be pulled inside. Who knows if we'd be allowed back out so easily.

"It's now or never." I look over at Mariëtte, who is still petting Bridget.

She looks down at the rabbit and tells her, "Ready or not, B. It's time."

We get out of the car and take in the iron gate. Somewhere beyond there is Stark. Somewhere else beyond there is Mills. I wonder if they've crossed paths yet. I wonder if they've made a plan. I wonder how close they might be to breaking out so I can see them again. I also wonder if they're even alive.

No, Liv, don't think like that. I suck in a breath and let it fill me up with oxygen. I feel my heart beat, knowing it's providing my organs with everything it needs. I can't explain it, but I get the feeling that the same thing is happening to both of them, too. They're there. I just need to make contact.

It's all up to you, Bridget.

"You've got the paper?" Mariëtte asks. I pull a tiny blank sheet of paper out of my pocket. Part of our testing was to find how much paper she would comfortably be willing to carry for longer periods of time. And this one in my hand is perfect rabbit mouth size.

"Got it right here," I tell her.

"I've got a pen in my purse if you need it," she offers. But I shake my head. A pen isn't secretive enough. I can't risk this rabbit leaving a handwritten note somewhere beyond that iron gate for someone else besides Stark to see.

"You done with your water?" I ask her instead.

She shrugs. "I guess so. There's a little bit left, but I didn't take you for a drink share-er."

Knowing there is about six billion bacteria in any person's mouth, I'm definitely not a drink share-er, but I'm not after a swig of water. I open up Mariëtte's door and take out the to-go drink in the holder. The top pops off easily and I tip it on its side so that any remaining liquid pours out.

"Hey!" Mariëtte yells.

"If you weren't done with it, you should have said so," I remind her.

All that's left inside is a few chunks of ice and the one thing I'm after — a slice of lemon.

I reach in and pull out the cold slice. I hold it in one hand while I put the plastic cup away.

"Is this part of your plan you didn't tell me about, Livvy?" The skepticism and intrigue are both clear in Mariëtte's words.

I run my fingers into my hair. It's wash day, anyway, so a little out of place curls won't be that big of a deal. I find one of the barretts I use to hold it back into a puff, unsnap it, and pull it out. I can already feel it sticking out of place. "You could say I've got a little secret. In fact, you gave me the idea."

"Olivia Landon, I have no idea what you're talking about."

I give her a smile. "It's all about citric acid." I put the small paper on the hood of the car and with the wide end of the clip in my hand, I dip the pointed end into the lemon. "I can use it as ink."

"Okay…" Again, I can hear Mariëtte doesn't understand, but she's following.

I make a single mark on the paper, then I blow on it to make sure it dries. "See?"

"I see nothing."

"Exactly. It dries clear, so you won't see anything. But if you add enough heat, it'll show up."

"Like invisible ink."

"Exactly. That way, if—" I stop and hold myself accountable to my words. "— *when* Stark finds it, he will be able to see the message. Anyone else won't blink an eye to it."

"And are you sure Stark would know what to do? You sure he won't see a blank paper like anyone else would? A piece of trash to throw away?"

I make a few more marks on the piece of paper in front of me, concentrating on which letters I've already made and which ones I need to make next.

"Guarantee it. He's the one that brought it up in the first place."

She looks at me, confused.

"What? Didn't I tell you? When he got our rabbit to leave notes for me out my door, I always sent them back with messages in invisible ink."

My smile mimics hers. Together, we crouch to the ground and settle Bridget down on the flat part of the dirt. I offer her the paper. She twitches her nose and accepts it, confused on where to go next. My hand reaches into my back pocket and pulls out a dried strawberry from Stark's granola stash.

I look Bridget into the eyes and mentally cross my fingers that she understands. "This is for you. But you need to find the man who needs that paper first, okay? When you come back, you get this." Her ears flicker in uncertainty. "And more!" I reach back into my pocket and show her that I have more to offer. "So much more. It'll be waiting for you when you get back. Promise. Just please, please deliver it safely. Okay?"

Bridget moves in a little semi-circle to face Mariëtte. Probably looking for snacks from her, too.

"You've got this, B. You're a good rabbit. You can do it. Just like Livvy said, come back safe, okay?"

As if Bridget understands, she moves again, this time facing the iron gate. She hops forward once, twice, and squeezes her body through the rungs. Then, she takes off. Faster than she ever did during training. Faster than I've ever seen her go. I hope she hears Stark's whistle and responds to it the same way she learned to respond to ours. She's a brave rabbit.

Or, perhaps, just motivated. I do have a lot of treats with me.

Mariëtte exhales when our bunny is out of sight. I didn't realize she was holding her breath. I wonder if she was doing it intentionally or if it took her by surprise, too.

"So, now what?" she asks.

"Now, we wait."

CHAPTER NINETEEN

Stark

Sixteen. I've counted sixteen cameras, all facing the make-shift morbid stage. Five pillars with pieces of art sitting within the dust of the dead. And with the amount that's still there, I again wonder how many No Names there actually are. And how many have gone missing. I close my eyes and think of all the faces I've seen and gotten to know. I can't say for sure how many have disappeared. I'm sure there's enough that several could be pulled aside for any minute wrongdoing and led straight into the crematorium to burn in the incinerator.

I hear several No Names work there. It's like doing a serial killer's dirty job for them. Out of all the horrors I've seen and done myself, at least I haven't had to actually harm a living person. All my nasty work has been done on the dead. Thank goodness, I haven't had to do anything like that since then.

The Supermoon is within a couple of days. Tomorrow is the test run. Which means if anyone is collecting names of the invited, they're doing it now.

I walk around the yard, inspecting where all the cameras are pointed. Interesting enough, none of them are aimed at Mills's mural. Of course not. Of course The Dignitary made sure the most beautiful part of this yard can't be seen by the mass public. Of course she wouldn't want to show off something real and moving. Of course the only things she cares about are the morbid curiosities she's forcing the artists to create. Everything that "needs" to be seen has to be manufactured by her ideals and suggestions.

Dali da Monet be damned.

I know exactly which paint strokes are from Mills's hands. When I touch my palm to it, I can almost feel her heartbeat speak through it. This is what true art is. It comes from the soul of the person making it, with the intention to touch others. The message itself has nothing to do with necessities of anything. It's just art for art's sake.

Because the person who made it wanted to. Because they put their heart into it. Because it's what they love to do, and they want to share that love in a visual medium so that others can enjoy it, too.

I hope Mills sees that, too. It'd kill me if she lost sight of her passion because someone else tried to redefine it.

I close my fist and shoot a look back up to the cameras posted on nearby trees and the sides of buildings. There are some I didn't catch before, but again, they're faced in different directions. They're pointed right in front of the displays, where I imagine chairs will line up as audience seats. I'm sure these are meant to catch reactions, see who might be brainwashed to believe this place would be a welcoming home to them. Counting these cameras, the number is now up to twenty. Plus six more that will no doubt record the commune guests coming and going.

"Wheet-woo," I let out a whistle and try to steady myself.

I walk circles around the area to double and triple check to make sure there aren't any more cameras I can find. None hidden in some weird hole in a tree. None halfway buried in the ground.

Confirmed. None of them are pointing at Mills's work. The reality hits me. Nor are there any pointing at the opening between the retaining wall and solitary confinement. There's nothing over in that direction at all.

According to these cameras, Mills doesn't exist. Nor does the beauty in her work.

"You must be one of the listers," a voice spooks me from behind. When I turn, I see a No Name I've never met before. I study his face. It's blank. Nothing discerning from it. Nothing that tells me anything of his personality or what it might have been like before this place got to him.

I'm so tired of naming the people who don't have any name. But I refuse to become just like everyone else here. I will not believe that these people don't have an identity. This is the same man I overheard being concerned about money. Clearly, his history has damaged him of being paid when he should.

Same, buddy. We've all had shitty jobs who cut corners on our paychecks.

I shouldn't assume, though. Whatever his trauma from the *banal* world, he's brought it here. I'll call him… McDuck, even though I'm sure he's not trying to be greedy. He just wants what he's due, and his eyes say that he's getting tired of not seeing it. His heart isn't even all in this job he's doing right in front of me.

In his hands is a stack of papers. He must have come from the paper mill. And the only reason why a No Name would be coming from there now would be…

"Yes, yes I am." I hold out my hand, ready to include my submission.

He hands me a pen and the top sheet of paper. Numbers one through fifteen are on the left margin. Over half of them are already written with a name and address on them. If there's one thing I can say about the MMS is that the people here work fast. Fast and diligent.

"I thought there were thirty seats?" I ask. Why isn't the sheet adding up?

"The Dignitary has decided to allow plus ones."

One of two things must be happening. Either The Dignitary's master plan is beyond what she's told us, and she's keeping extra secrets to herself. Or, what's more likely, she's slipping. I'm willing to bet that she doesn't have as tight of a grip on everything laid out in front of her like she'd like us all to believe.

Either way, convenience has given me the gift of placing this particular No Name in my path right here, right now. And I am taking one of those spots regardless if I'm a "lister" or not.

Quickly, I scrawl the only name I have in mind and the address to match.

Without even thinking about it, I let out another nervous whistle. "Wheet-woo." It's like relief just left me as I hand the pen and paper back to the man in front of me.

"Thank you. On to the next." McDuck waves goodbye at me, and I turn my attention back to Mills's painting. It's a damn shame that she was forced to confine her talents. She deserves to have a place that will let it loose. So she can enjoy it, love it, and simply do it because it's the thing that lives in her heart.

A rustling sound tickles my ears. I turn around to see what it is. Nothing, I suppose. The No Name that was here is gone, off to find more people without names to write down the names of others. Seems ridiculous now that I think of it that way. No one else is around that I can see.

I scan the trees again, looking for the tell-tale signs of metal boxes to see if I missed any cameras on my other searches.

Again, the rustling sound. Oddly enough, the rhythm of it is familiar. I just can't seem to place what it is. Another search around and I still don't see anyone or anything. I half expect someone to jump scare me, pop out of hiding and see how far they can make me jump into the air.

What if someone saw me write on that list? Someone who knows I wasn't supposed to? Would I get manhandled and thrown into solitary confinement just like Mills and Paula? I'd have to make a break for it, and then what would happen to Mills?

The rustling sounds closer now. Almost like it can touch me.

What if it's someone like Bugs? Or Bugs himself? He'd get a complete kick out of catching me in the act of doing something I'm not supposed to be doing. He'd tote me away to The Dignitary herself, presenting me like a cat who caught a prize mouse.

Or a rabbit who caught a dandelion snack.

A rabbit.

My eyes find where the noise is coming from. And it's not Bugs at all. Nor is it any other excited man in a linen jumpsuit.

It's a little gray rabbit with a twitchy pink nose. A warm feeling hits my heart like a dart. She looks just like the bunny Livvy and I had growing up, Harriet. Only, she's got an extra patch of white, right above her tail.

I bend down to get a closer look at her. "Where did you come from?" I ask the rabbit. She looks up at me and tilts her ears a little. I give her a smile, and almost as a response, she bends her head back down to drop something at my feet.

A piece of paper.

"So, you do know Livvy." She didn't forget the rabbit hole at all. She found a new one to use, and trained it just like I did with Harriet. My sister is brilliant.

I pick up my gift and unfold the note. Nothing on it.

Of course there's nothing on it.

I clasp the paper between the palms of my hands. The average body temperature is ninety-eight degrees. Probably not enough to activate the invisible ink message, but definitely enough to try.

Placing my mouth over my thumbs, I blow hot air into my clasped hands. It stays trapped in there for a few seconds, then leaks out. When I feel the air cool down, I do it again. And again. A silent prayer helps me to open my hands and look.

It's not supposed to work. It should take more heat. And yet, when I reveal the paper in my hands, there's a message clear as day.

Found the rabbit hole.

It's a good thing I wrote her name on that invitation list.

CHAPTER TWENTY

Mills

The light through the crack in the door tells me it's morning. Or, at least, it's not night. I can see the blanket that was left for me a little clearer, and I'm glad I didn't snuggle up with it. The smell that radiates from it tells me the dark green color isn't just the shade of yarn it's made of.

I did fall asleep sometime between being shoved in here and now. So I'm guessing it's been twenty-four hours. I have no idea how long they're planning on keeping me like this, but it can't possibly be too long. There's only a tiny slot in the door. I guess it could be for food and water, but I don't know how much would actually fit in there. It's more like a mail slot. An envelope might fit. Or a hand with a key. But a tray of food would be pushing it with its width.

Maybe that's their plan. Maybe they plan on keeping me locked up until they forget about me and I die on my own. Starvation, dehydration, and completely and utterly on my own. I slam my hand on the dirty wall. Those jerks probably can't even hear that. If they had, they're ignoring it.

My throat is scratchy from yelling out as much as I could. Paula didn't answer my screamed apologies. Neither did anyone else. I'm going to end up rotting away out of sight.

Out of sight, out of mind. I'm not their problem if they can't see it.

Even the birds seem unbothered. Somewhere beyond these walls, birds are chirping away, singing about their day. They're probably jumping from tree to tree, playing some game of freedom tag I don't have access to.

Freedom. It's such an odd word, isn't it? One moment, I feel free as a bird and the next, I'm trapped in a cage. This place is screwing with my mind. I love it. I hate it. I adore it. These are my people. I don't know who my people are.

Dali da Monet understands. He, She, They, understands. The collective is there to guide me, standing behind me, ready to help and support me. That's how this works. A higher power is above me, ready to show me the way as long as I'm open to hearing it, right? That's how all this works, right? It has to be.

Just like the other artists here. They get it. We're all striving to be who we're supposed to be. Ready to find and live out our purpose so our souls and expression can be saved for the next realm of life, death, and everything in between.

We're all ready to hear Dali da Monet. We're all waiting. We're all eager to be used for her work. Their work.

But then why am I shoved into a hot box in the middle of nowhere?

I breathe in and out deliberately. Out goes all the animosity I carried with me here. All the anger that came up and frustration that's boiled underneath. I don't need any of that. It's all as helpful as a hole in the head.

Like the one I feel is developing right now. Leaky-leaky, there it all goes.

And I breathe in everything that's meant for me. A place to belong. A supportive network. A love for art and the attachment to creation. The messages are there. It's all there. I'm ready for the artistic ancestors to speak through me and allow it all out.

But isn't that what I did? That's what I thought I did.

I guess not, though.

So, what is it? What should I be doing? What should I have done?

I slump down to the floor. I've already been here enough times within the hours I've been confined. The dirt is welcome. It's my canvas. My hand moves over it, creating a new blank space, and use my finger to draw. Just squiggles. Enough to feel a design happen in front of me.

It feels right, just letting it happen.

It feels wrong because it's not what I was told to do.

Out of frustration, I wipe away my doodles. It shouldn't exist. Not here, not now. It's not part of saving the world. There's no message in it. There's no intention. It just existed.

Not anymore. Done. Gone.

My back hits the door. I wish I could push it open. For a moment, I try. I throw myself backward just to see if I can make it work. Maybe break it off the hinges.

It doesn't budge. Clearly I'm not strong enough. If only Livvy were here.

If only Livvy were alive.

If only I hadn't left her body where I had found it.

If only Noland hadn't gotten to her the way he got to all those other girls.

There he is again. Noland, slipping into my thoughts, making me hate him and love him all over again. I suppose that's what family does, huh? They mess with your emotions up, down, left, right, front, and center. Forgive and forget, right?

I could never forget Livvy, though. If she were here right now, she'd be able to shove herself through the door and break me out. And then what? Where would I go? Back to my room where I could quietly wait until the next set of instructions? I'm not sure I belong there anymore. Not as a girl who went off, gallivanting to create her own set of rules like she owns the place.

I smack myself on the side of my head. *Stupid Mills. You don't own anything. This was never your call.*

I take a few moments to simply sit. There's nothing else to do here but sit. Creating seems wrong. Thinking seems wrong. Attempting to meditate and call on Dali da Monet is definitely wrong. I'm not there yet. At this point, I'm not sure I'll ever be.

More birds make their calls. Let them play their games. Let them have fun. There's no place for me doing that either. And another bird hops on the ground. Or, at least that's what it sounds like.

Only this bird is loud. It must have heavy feet. It's dragging steps out as if it's making large, slow steps.

That's no bird. That's a person.

Hours earlier, I would have slammed my fists repeatedly on the wall. I would have called out. I would have gotten that person's attention, whatever it would take.

I don't deserve that attention. Not right now. No matter how much my heart second guesses it. My heart makes my mouth speak, anyway. "Livvy, Paula, I'm so sorry."

The heavy-footed bird-person stops.

"Mills?" The sound doesn't even make sense to me. My name? Who would be out there to call my name?

I turn to face the door I've been leaning against and move my eyes to the would-be-food slit. There isn't much I can see. A pair of legs inside a canvas jumpsuit. One of a million in these parts.

"Mills?" The voice is quiet, almost unrecognizable. And had I not spent time with it one-on-one I wouldn't even give it a second thought.

But I know that voice. And when it calls again, it feels like she's right outside the door, like she's touching it.

I put my hand on my side of the door, wondering if she's on the other side doing the same.

"Paula, is that really you?" My own voice feels foreign. It's scratchy and slow. It definitely belongs in someone else's mouth. Not mine.

"Mills, you are in there. I'm so glad." She's like a whisper. She always has been. But that whisper is alive and well. And it's not caged in. That whisper is free, just like the birds playing their games.

My entire body feels relieved. Every bit of tension I held onto because I put her in a solitary hot box on her own is gone. But then my stomach jumps in my throat. Why is she out? What is it that got her out of that box and into the open air? How did she gain the freedom I may not even deserve?

"Paula, are you okay? What happened?"

There's a silence that follows, and my heart can't take it. "Paula? Please tell me you're okay." My words are pleading. Begging. I really don't want her time locked away to have damaged her at all.

"Mills, I'm definitely okay." I can feel her smile even through the barriers between us. "Mills, they came to get me. They said my time was up and ready. It's my time to shine, Mills. They're ready for me to do what I need to do."

I don't understand what she's saying. What does it mean that it's her time?

"They told me it's just like my handler. She played a huge part in all of this. I imagine yours did, too."

Noland? He played a huge part? I haven't even seen him out of his room in... forever. Who knows what that man is doing behind closed doors. But I guess if it's all for the sake of the ascension date, then whatever he's done is worth it, right?

"Now it's my turn. They're calling me in. And I'm ready. But there's one thing."

Confusion runs through me. "Paula, what thing? What are you talking about?"

There's movement in front of the little slit in the door. In slides her flat hand, holding something lumpy and flesh-like.

No. Not flesh *like*. Fleshy.

A fleshy lump that should be attached to the side of her head. The slit in her door must not have been for food after all. It must have been for a sharpened blade, giving Paula the choice to do what she wanted with it.

"Paula, is that…?"

"It's an offering, Mills. Just like Van Gogh. My right ear. They needed to know I was serious about my commitment to my role. And I am. I so am, Mills." She pauses, and I watch her fingers caress the lobe laying down on her palm. "They gave me a choice. I could either sit in the box and wait to be used when they were ready for me, or I could show my allegiance in a way the ancestral greats would approve. This was it, Mills. And now I'm ready."

Her hand disappears from sight. I imagine just a few feet away, she pockets her own ear, jagged bloody bits and all.

"Mills." Her voice is a little stronger now, more confident. "Mills, I have a place here. They're assuring me of it. I'm ready, I'm so ready. Dali da Monet is coming for me, and I've never been so elated and reassured at the same time. My place is here. We may have fallen off track for a minute, but that was only a blip. A silly blip, Mills. Hang in there. Your turn will come soon. They'll be ready for you, too, okay? Just hang in there until they can give you the choice, too."

With that, she's gone. The legs I can see from the little slit walk out of sight. I'm alone again. Alone with the thought about what Paula just told me.

And her ear in her hand.

They're going to give me a choice, and I need to think about what choice I'll make. Either refuse to budge and rot away, just as I expected they were doing to begin with. Or make an offering that the artistic ancestors like Vincent Van Gogh would appreciate.

My fingernails aren't long, but I use what I have to pinch the back of my ear, right about the same place Paula would have had to hack away. It stings. Hurts. Sawing it off wouldn't be fun.

I breathe in all of what makes sense. The approval. The necessity. The need for art to make sense.

It wouldn't be fun at all, but I could do it. If it was in the name of Dali da Monet and literally saving the world, I could sacrifice a single ear to make it happen. It would be my gift I'd gladly give up.

CHAPTER TWENTY-ONE

Stark

A sour pit forms in my stomach. The tiny thing in my hand kickstarted that uncomfortable feeling and it's had a hold on me since. I squeeze my hand tightly, thinking if I do so tight enough, it'll turn the item into something else, something better, much like pressure turns coal into a diamond.

But nothing happens. Absolutely nothing. The glass bottle with a single pill is still in my hands.

I've been tasked with a job I equally want and don't want, to deliver this pill to the poor girl I put in solitary confinement. Paula. She's right behind the door in front of me, waiting for my arrival. My entire job is to knock and hand it over. There's a line or two I've been told to memorize.

I won't be able to speak them, though. I'm not even sure I'll be able to hand it over.

It's death. This little pill is death. Cyanide, probably.

But that's not what they call it here. They call it an enlightenment pill. And everyone who doesn't ascend on the specified Supermoon gets the delightful opportunity to achieve a lesser form of enlightenment first.

It makes me sick.

Why I'm chosen to do this job is beyond me. I hear Doctor James is usually the person to do it. But he's been missing for some time now and I have no idea where he's gone off to.

I swallow down a lump. Those piles of ash on display are getting bigger every time I walk past. I wonder if one of those has his name on it. I already know it's more than the No Names who are being sacrificed. It's also all of the people who end up with a lesser enlightenment before the show airs to the public. Or at least the pieces of them that won't be used as supplies.

A flash of blood red washes over my eyes. My palms itch thinking about the way the slivers of skin felt inside of them. Once Paula takes this, she'll be on a butcher rack, too.

But there's a piece of me that's glad I was assigned this horrendous task. I wasn't able to convince her to run earlier, but maybe with this position, I'll be able to convince her otherwise. Maybe I can talk some sense into her. With the right look or the right set of words, I might be able to save Paula still.

I look down the hall to the left, then to the right. Two cameras are pointing in my direction. I can't not at least knock.

Holding my breath, I tap the door with my fist. Secretly, I hope she doesn't answer. Maybe she's out, enjoying a sit under the trees. Or maybe she fell asleep and she doesn't hear me at all. Maybe she's so wrapped up in some sort of artistic stupor, elated that she's reached a certain freedom by coming out of solitary.

The doorknob turns. No such luck.

My breath hitches when the door opens. Paula's gaze is straightforward, her hair out of her face. She's not the shy, unconfident girl I led toward that shed. She's self-assured, making eye contact, and smiling.

She really was expecting me. I assume whoever led her out of her confinement explained it all. They told her I'd be here with a gift. And they told her that taking the gift would mean reaching everything she ever wanted.

I hate this so much.

She tilts her head and I realize that the side of it is bandaged up in gauze and tape. Her ear. I heard some No Names talk about leaving solitary confinement. The one requirement is that the prisoner needs to sacrifice a piece of themselves.

My naivety wanted to believe that meant something more ominous and less destructive. Something like renouncing a belief or something like that.

I guess again, I'm wrong. They really did mean a piece of yourself. She gave up her ear.

And unless I can convince her otherwise, she's about to give up a whole lot more.

The sour feeling in my stomach grows from a small ball to a giant boulder. I can't even seem to get a word out. Not even a hello. I glance over at one of the cameras aimed at me and force a smile at Paula.

Her smile grows wider. "Hi," she says. "I hear you're giving me a gift?"

I take a few moments to gather up my thoughts. What do I say to her? I can't give over this bottle. She's a confused girl, not some sacrificial animal. My fist grows tight around the bottle and I can't find the right words to say. "I'm supposed to give you a gift," I tell her. It's true. I'm supposed to. I don't want to, not this anyway. What's in my hand isn't a gift.

"So, where is it? Where is my enlightenment gift?"

The poor girl looks so eager, excited. She's been fed so many lies. What can I say to break her from them?

"Listen, Paula, right?"

At her name, she looks confused. She knits her eyebrows and tilts her head. Her eyes take me in, scanning my facial features for something recognizable.

I suppose when we become No Names, there's no piece of identity left to any of the artists we serve. Not even differences in our features.

We all get wiped clean, like we don't even exist. She doesn't remember me from before. She doesn't realize I'm the guy who tried to get her to run and save herself.

"I know this place is confusing to you, but listen." I look around me to make sure no one else is coming down the hall to check my work over my shoulder. It's all clear. "Whatever you think they're all promising you here is wrong."

Good job, Stark. It's a good start.

"They? You mean you?" Paula's timid finger points at the little jar in my hand. "You came here with a promise, didn't you?"

I didn't even realize my palm was open, with the single pill on display. "I-I…" I stammer. How do I explain this to her in a way that would make any sense?

"Isn't that what that is?" Her soft voice doesn't even hide her eagerness. "The promise to a better reality?" She inches closer to me, and I move my hand further back. She can't grab this. She can't take it. I have the chance to save her life, if I can just find the right words to tell her.

"It's - it's not what you think." The sour pit in my stomach is turning even more. "What I mean is that the promise they've been telling you… it's not true. It's dangerous, Paula."

"Dali da Monet says it's perfection." She takes another step toward me, and I pull away a little more.

"Dali da Monet doesn't-" I hear footsteps down the hallway and lower my voice. "Look, Dali da Monet doesn't exist. It's not a real thing. And you can't take this pill. It's not going to give you what you think it will."

The footsteps grow closer. I don't have time to see who it is or how far away they are. I only have time to make sure the few words I can get out count.

"Paula, this pill isn't medicine or a cure or anything like that." My words aren't getting through to her. She looks as confused as ever. "Paula, this pill is-"

"The next step to your everlasting future."

Shivers ripple down my spine and my lips clench shut. The voice behind me sets me in paralyzed fear. I know that voice.

Painfully, I swallow down my fear and slowly turn around.

"Thank you for your help. I'll take it from here." The Dignitary puts one hand on my arm and the other in my palm. She clasps her fingers around the bottle and lifts it out of my grasp. It's literally out of my hands now. Everything. The bottle, the pill, the situation.

I want to yell; push this woman out of the way and run. I want to pull Paula into safety where we can both chase down Mills and all get off of this commune so we can pretend none of this ever happened.

But that's the exact reason why I can't. That's the exact reason why my body is paused in position. I don't want Paula to get hurt, but I need Mills out. I need her like I need oxygen, and I'm too afraid that if I do anything, I'll never get to breathe in her scent again. I can't move. I can't say anything. I can't do anything. Except watch The Dignitary unscrew the top of the little bottle and dump it out into her hand. She walks over to Paula, who stares back, wide-eyed and hungry.

It seems like full minutes are passing by, but it's only split seconds.

And The Dignitary shows off the little pill between her two fingers inches away from Paula's eyes. All I can do is whisper, "No," but it doesn't do any good.

The Dignitary's hands move to Paula's mouth and before I know it, the little pill slips between her lips and disappears.

Paula swallows and closes her eyes.

Everything in me sinks as I watch her pull the ends of her mouth into a quiet smile.

I know the truth, though. It won't take long before that quiet smile is no longer quiet. She'll thrash around while her insides will eat away at themselves. She'll vomit in excruciating pain. She'll tear herself apart as her body breaks down.

Cyanide isn't pretty. Neither are the lies that have been fed to her.

The Dignitary turns around, faces me. Without a word, she steps forward as if I wasn't even standing there. She pushes me out the door and within a few steps, the two of us are in the hallway and she closes the door shut behind us.

Her face is stoic, still. I can't tell if she knows what I was about to do or not. I can't read her expression at all. She gives me one blank look, staring straight into my eyes. I swear I can feel them burn.

"Let her go."

With those three words, she's gone.

And I am, too.

CHAPTER TWENTY-TWO

The Dignitary

I'm losing it. I'm losing all of it. I feel like I'm swimming in a pool of a thousand problems and I can't find my way out of it. I'm drowning and I don't know why. I used to have things under control. There was a time when everything was snugly under my thumb. It's no longer fitting in a tightly wound spot. It's spilling out, and around me. Everywhere I can't reach to pull it back in.

A million questions swirl through my head and bang around against my brain like ping-pong balls.

I've got to get out of here. I've got to find solace.

I've got to talk to Dali da Monet and figure out exactly what the hell is going on. Why everything is falling apart.

Making my way to the staircase, I let myself up on the next floor and the next. When I get to my floor, I scan myself in and verbally check in with three No Name guards. They've manned this post since they arrived here and haven't left.

At least I think it's the same men. Now that I'm thinking about it, they may have switched out once or twice. One seems to have a beard. I don't remember any facial hair. And another has piercing blue eyes. Wouldn't I have remembered that shade looking back at me during a check-in? Who knows. It's not like I can keep up with what they're all doing when they're all the same anyway.

Which is the exact problem I'm facing now.

Shit. Shit. Shit. Shit.

There was once a point when I could keep track of it all. I knew everyone's face and position. I could snap my fingers and they'd all jump in line quicker than my fingers could part of each other. I had it all under control, knowing who is doing what in the tight ship I call Memento Mori. For fuck's sake, I changed my name for it.

I had all the dials set to forward. Everyone was tuned into me. There wasn't a single move that was made that wasn't carefully calculated by my watch, all for the same reason.

For my enlightenment.

Sure, theirs, too, but I lived enough trauma in my life to deserve it the most. You don't live through a drug addict mother who nearly sold you off to her boyfriends when they got tired of her for nothing. Not even the *best* foster care experiences can erase that.

So, yeah, I earned my place in a better afterlife. And I'll be damned if I don't get there because of someone else's fuck-ups.

And now? I barely know who is who and where they're going. No Names are choosing their own tasks. They're talking behind my back. They're making decisions without checking in and walking to the beat of a drum I thought I took away from them the moment they stepped foot in my society. Even more unbelievable, they're questioning all my motives and the truths that I tell them.

I spent my life before MMS learning the truths. I sat down and talked to Dali da Monet. I meditated. I cleansed. I beat myself up, tore my old identity apart, and built up a new one that actually *means something in this world*. I did all the hard work so none of these people would ever have to. All they need to do is sit back and listen to instructions. How hard is that?

I've even heard some of these lowly No Name have even whispered questions about their payments.

They're worried about *money*. Money! Even if Dali da Monet needs a toll before we enter the next realm, it's not like any of those fools will need it. They're where they need to be. Serving us.

Serving me.

I wave my hand to dismiss the guardsmen in front of me and make my way into my room. The only area in this whole damn place where I can truly block everything out.

My room is quiet. Simple. It's its own blank canvas without anything on the walls including windows. It's how I like it. I'm not the artist of my own life after all. That's all up to the highest power. What things look like is their call. I'm just a vessel to carry out her cause. I welcome myself onto the floor and spread out like a starfish. *Dali da Monet, please come to me. Speak to me. Tell me where I've gone wrong so I can fix it.*

Everything is happening all at once. The Supermoon is coming and I'm not prepared at all.

The computers aren't working. The artistry isn't done. Every time I check on The Circle members, I see more and more people struggling with a medium they should know just as well as the back of their hands. Two of my suppliers threw themselves into solitary after going completely rogue. And now I have no idea what that last No Name was up to. He was supposed to deliver an enlightenment pill and I caught him delivering… a *speech*?

I could have thrown him in the incinerator.

Maybe I should have.

But I didn't. I choked, freaked out, and ran from that room straight here. If things are dripping out of my hands, I need to check in with the ancestral greats. They haven't steered me wrong yet, and, clearly, my human self isn't to be relied on. I'm derailing myself with every turn I take.

Besides, if I need to throw him into the incinerator, I have time, right? I can use one of the other No Names to take him there. Or rather, take someone there. That's what those men are there for. They can get rid of the problem for me.

But, is he the problem?

I clench every muscle in my body. Or am I the problem?

Shit. Shit. Shit.

Time is creeping up on me so quickly, too quickly, I need to know I'm not losing my mind. I need to know I'm still on track.

Dali da Monet. Speak to me now.

My fingers rake the carpet under me as I call in the collective. Every fiber of the carpet flips under my touch, tickling my skin, and I call Her name.

"Dali da Monet."

Nothing.

"Dali da Monet, come to me."

When I don't hear an answer, I let my palms rest where they are. Maybe if I stay still She'll come. They've always said patience is the key. You need patience to get what you want. But I'm losing my patience, and I don't know how to get it back when everything seems to be flooding away from me.

"Please, Dali da Monet. Please come speak to me."

Every moment that passes, I play all the mistakes over and over in my mind. Every little hiccup that should have never happened I had let slip out and drift away.

My feet kick at the floor. This is my fault. Everything here is my fault. I've done this to myself and now I've agreed to some bullshit test show for what? So outsiders can come in and see what's happening behind closed doors before the real Supermoon show starts?

What's that going to do? Nothing. It doesn't even seem feasible at this point to even do it. So why did I agree? Because I thought I heard Dali da Monet speak?

Please. She didn't speak to me. I just needed an answer. Something to move everyone forward because I said so. And now, I'm paying the price for it.

"Argghhh!" I slam my head against the floor. "Dali da Monet, come save me! Show me how to be. Give me guidance so we can ascend and stand with you."

I don't care if anyone can hear me. What are they going to do? Tell on me? To whom? I'm the only person who's really calling the shots. There's no one above my grade to run to.

"Ha!" I force out even louder. "Ha! Ha! HA!" Forcing out fake laughter strikes me as funny. Tiny giggles spill out of me and into the room. Giggles turn into chuckles. Chuckles morph into snickers and snickers into loud, barking cackles.

My stomach tenses and aches as I roll into a ball on the floor.

It's hilarious. Absolutely hilarious.

Here I am, entering the only position I've ever wanted to be in. And yet everything is slipping away into space itself.

Slipping away like the moon and stars.

Super.

Like the Supermoon.

Everything inside of me bursts into fits. My stomach hasn't felt this tense from laughter in a very long time.

I wish I could enjoy it for longer, but I came here for a purpose.

I came here to talk to Dali da Monet. And They aren't speaking.

My body tenses up one more time, then relieves itself of everything I'm holding to make way for the collective voices I'm waiting for.

I just want to get my shit straight. So I can actually concentrate on the pieces I need to. So I can make everything perfect.

For Dali da Monet. But for me, as well. Especially for me.

CHAPTER TWENTY-THREE

Stark

I run. I run as fast as I can. The Dignitary left me without any word of where she was going or what she saw. Or didn't see. Or hear. Which is terrifyingly lucky.

My fingers are crossed she didn't hear me try to talk Paula into running away.

Though my heavy heart wishes I did it better. I wish I could have said more, push Paula out of that room, and lead her to her own freedom. I hate myself for not doing so. I'd probably hate myself more if I didn't at least give myself the chance to save Mills.

Who knows how long I have before I'm pulled aside and questioned. The Dignitary could easily turn around and come back after me. Or any one of these insane No Names could easily decide I should be thrown into the dust-creator if they get word I was going against orders. I still don't even know where the incinerator is.

But I do know where solitary is. And I know Mills is somewhere beyond those trees.

I erase the image in my head of Paula. Her assuming expression makes my stomach turn over and over. I hate that she believed every lie that was fed to her, including the last pill that was shoved down her throat.

Willingly. I have to keep in mind it was willingly. She wanted it to happen.

Ugh, I hate this. I tell the acid in my stomach that there has to be some solace in that, regardless of how awful it was. There's some hope that as it ate away at her from the inside out, the lies gave her some kind of fictional peace.

Look at me, telling myself lies to try and make the horrors in front of me a little less bitter. There's no peace in cyanide. I swallow back the acid that threatens to spill out. I know Paula's death wasn't peaceful, and I'll forever carry the weight of guilt on my shoulders for being a part of it.

But I can't focus on her now. That will only slow me down. And I can't let it slow me down. My feet have to move fast and my head has to move faster. Paula's story is said and done. Mills's isn't. Mills's story is still being written, and I have to believe I can help her with a better ending. There isn't enough time to do anything else but try to save her.

I reach the line of trees past the layout for the show, past any of the strung up cameras, past everything most of the commune traffic travels, and I reach the solitary buildings. Looking at each of these in a neat row, they don't look much bigger than outhouses. How can anyone survive in that for any length of time? It's barely enough to stretch out comfortably. At least not at my six-foot-two frame.

My body clenches when I reach the room where we left Paula. This is the last place where she was whole, where she had a chance to break out before she was broken enough to never be fixed. I place my hand on the door, then clench it into a fist. "I'm sorry I couldn't help you," I whisper out loud.

But I can't stay long. I can't afford to feel bad about what I could have done and didn't because Mills is waiting for me, whether she knows it or not.

I walk to the next building and knock. "Mills?" I ask, but no one answers. I move on to the next "Mills!" I say a little louder, and again no one answers. I move on again and again. At the last tiny building, I suck in a deep breath and ask again, "Mills?"

Rustling comes from the other side of the door. She's in there. She has to be in there.

"Mills! Is that you? Are you okay?"

She doesn't answer me in words, but I can hear more movement. I take a single step back to compose myself. Something dark moves in front of the little slit of an opening, and it makes my heart thump a heavy beat.

I drop to my knees to see better. Staring back at me are two piercing eyes void of any emotion.

"Mills!" My heart beats itself into my throat. "It's so good to finally see you." I swallow back the lump that's formed. "Not like this, but I'm glad to see you. What I can see of you. Oh, Mills, are you okay?"

She blinks once, twice, and then does a little fluttering thing with her eyelids. When they finally clear up, her eyes are wet and shiny. Tears collect on the insides of them, and the sight of her emotion forces my hands to jolt up to the door. They ring the metal with a bang.

The sudden movement makes her flinch. "I'm so sorry, Mills." I make a gentler pat on the door. "For scaring you and for you being in there. I swear, I'm going to get you out, okay? I'm going to get you somewhere safe."

She gives a slow blink, like she's not fully awake. "I know I've thought crazy things before, but I must be going out of my mind. You can't be who I think you are." Her words are slow, but I can hear the wit hiding under the tired words and sluggish speech. She may have been torn to the bare minimum, but I can hear a little bit of Mills-ness that's there. Of course she's a fighter.

I give her a little chuckle. "Mills, I'm not sure about crazy, but it's me, Stark."

Her eyes close and she shakes her head. "You can't get me out of here. I'm being punished. I wasn't supposed to stray away, do what I wanted. I should have been a good girl and stayed in my room. I should have waited behind closed doors, quiet until given a new direction. Just like Noland's been doing."

"Noland? Noland!" I clench my jaw at the thought of that man. But then again, if she's fallen for whatever penance this cult has fed her, I don't want her to think I'm angry at her, as well. "Mills, Noland was an ass. Don't you remember hating him because of that? He killed those girls around campus. He trapped them, raped them, and killed them. And what's worse is that you were supposed to be one of them. Mills, remember what he did to you. Remember what happened. Remember how awful that man was."

She blinks again, and I can see it. It's just a flicker, but her fire is there. She's remembering.

"But for whatever demented reason, you didn't end up like those other girls. If there's anything I can be thankful for, it's that he didn't kill you, too. But he did drag you here. In this nasty cult. But, Mills, I can't let you stay here. If you do, they will kill you. You'll end up just like those girls, the missing No Names, and Noland himself."

The flicker of the fire in her eyes waves. I can tell, she doesn't quite get it.

"Mills, Noland is dead. He ran his course as a serial killer, attacked Livvy outside your house, and fed you heart-first into this brainwashing cult. And now he's dead. As horrible as he was, he's not what you have to worry about anymore. He's not the big bad at the head of all of this. The belief system in this cult, how they've all tried to break you is. The Dignitary is. But I will not. Will. Not. Allow you to continue in this place anymore."

Her eyes look confused, brows scrunched together. "Dead? Wait, no, don't you mean he's gone to his ascension?" Her words are slightly stronger, trying to make sense of what I've told her.

"Ascension?" She's deeper in the lies than I even thought. "Mills, no. He's dead. Gone. No more. I'd say six feet underground, but he's actually in a box, torn to shreds to be used as art himself. Honestly, saying it out loud, it's too good for him. It's too good for someone who did this to you."

I swallow everything back and readjust my weight. I don't have the time to break all the brainwashing this cult has done, but I can at least break the honest truth to her.

"Mills, listen. I need to find a way to get you out of here, but we can't do it now. We can't run out of the commune without someone chasing us down. We need a ride out. I have a plan, and I have a feeling while we're waiting someone else is going to try and get to you before me. You can't let that happen, okay? If anyone comes by, stand your ground. Don't let them come in. Kick them in the balls if you need to. I promise, I'll find my way to you and we'll get the hell out of here."

She breaks eye contact from me. "Paula said they'll let me out if I offer them a gift."

I slam my fist on the door and she flinches again. "Absolutely not, Mills. You owe this place nothing more than a wave of a middle finger in the air. No gifts from you. Do not give any more of yourself to this hellhole."

She scoffs. Just a little more of herself is coming out. It makes my insides flutter.

Her eyes roll and sarcasm drips from her mouth, "But it's what Dali da Monet wants, isn't it?"

If I never have to listen to that name again, I'll be one happy man. "Listen, if there is any higher power looking over us all, guiding us on this Earth and anywhere in the afterlife, I have to believe that higher power is full of love. Love, Mills. I can't believe this place has anyone thinking anything else." I lick my drying lips so they don't crack under stress. "Love wants to see you survive, here. Now. And all of this? It's not love, Mills. Let's prove to them that love wins. Every time. Not whatever shit they've been pushing."

She's silent for a moment, then locks her gaze back onto mine. "If you really are Stark, then I'm so sorry about Livvy. I miss her."

Livvy. That's right, Mills doesn't know that Livvy survived Noland's attempted murder. Then this might be the news that will save her after all.

"Mills, Livvy's alive."

Her eyes dart left and right. I can tell, she's not sure if she believes me. She wants to, but that little flame in her eyes doesn't know if it can become a full blaze or if it should dim out.

"Listen, Livvy's alive. She's fine. In fact, she's part of my plan. She's coming tomorrow."

She shakes her head in disbelief. "She's our getaway car?"

I wish I could reach inside this little gap in the door and hug her. All I can do is hope my laugh reaches her heart instead. "She's our getaway car."

Her wet eyes can't hold the tears in any longer. They drip down her face out of my sight. "Livvy's alive?" I don't know how much she actually believes me.

My own tears match hers, and I nod my head. "Yes! She's alive. Mills, Livvy misses you, too. And I - I miss you. Mills, promise me you'll come back to us, okay? We're going to do all we can to bring you back home. Away from this living nightmare. I just need you to be you, okay? The real you, not whatever dulled version they think they have."

"Livvy's alive." She blinks away more tears. "Livvy's alive." It's like she's reprogramming herself right in front of my eyes. "Livvy's. Alive."

I wish I could hold her. I want to pull her close, hug her. I want to bring her to my sister and watch her face light up. I want to see life and snark and all the Mills witticisms I love so much come back to her. Fully.

She nods. I can't wait to see her snark back at one hundred percent.
"Stark?"
I move even closer to the slit in the door. "Yes?"
"Stark, if that really is you… I miss you, too."

CHAPTER TWENTY-FOUR

The Dignitary

Okay, okay, okay. So Dali da Monet didn't come to me. She didn't speak to me. They didn't say anything. It's not the end of the world. Not yet. It's fine.

I'm fine. Everything's fine.

We just have to make sure tonight's trial run goes off without a hitch. Because that's the test, right? See if it's all going to work? See if things are all set for the real deal? That's what the intention is anyway. Right?

But my freaking artists, The Circle, they haven't completed all of their work yet. They're still lollygagging around as if there's nothing riding on it. As if we're in some stupid art camp where they can play fiddlesticks with themselves, giggle, and treat their art like hobbies. *Hobbies.* And because the way time is speeding past, there are still several more artists who haven't even had a chance to *test* those supplies yet.

It's not like they all can the way they're supposed to anyway. We'll have to make due. Get innovative. A woman's job is never fully done.

I know what we need to do. We need to speed up the process. Make it happen. If the higher power ancestors don't answer me, I have to create an answer myself. Sacrifices one through four have already fulfilled their purpose. It's time to speed it up even faster. Make sure my artists have enough time to destroy, create, and call in what's needed.

Screw the original plan. What does a schedule have to do with destiny anyway?

I knock on the boy's door. The eager one who's been fantastic at taking orders. And I'm sure when he's ready, he'll be fantastic at giving them and making all the calls a good leader needs to.

This feels right, doesn't it? Choosing a new Dignitary to lead the way after me? I mean, it makes sense to keep it going after I move on to the next realm.

I'm sure Dali da Monet would be fine with it, right?

It seems fine. It feels fine.

It's fine.

I'm sure They would be happy for me. At me.

He opens up the door. He's like a kid walking into a candy store, full of wonder when he sees me.

I exhale the tension I've been carrying. This is why I do this. For artists like this, who know what to appreciate, especially when it's right in front of them.

"Zak, right? Isn't that your name?"

He gives an enthusiastic nod. "That's me!"

"Zak, I have something to ask of you."

He looks confused, but swings the door wider so I can come in.

He leads me to the sitting area and we both find a relaxing place to rest. I should have brought my tea, but these days I'm lucky if I remember where I'm even going.

"Zak, you believe in the power of Dali da Monet, right?"

He gives me a shy smile. "Of course, Dignitary. I believe it with my entire body."

"Please, call me Iris." I'm not sure when I started letting my realm of reality name slip, but every time it does, it feels like I'm barely holding onto a piece of my slipping confidence.

"Iris," he tries it out. The way his lips turn up, I can tell he likes saying my name. I like the sound of it, too. "What is it you needed to ask me?"

I'm not so sure I should make such a big request right out of the gate. So, instead, I break the ice with something I know he's looking forward to.

"First of all, have you been enjoying your new materials?"

He frowns. "I don't have any new materials, Iris."

Shit. I frown back. "What do you mean?"

He looks at his door, with the number seven on it. "We haven't gotten to my number yet. Last I heard, they had to drag out materials number four out of solitary. There are still a couple more who have to fall into their own self-sacrifice before we get to my materials."

I think about what he's saying. There are so many people to keep track of. Who was number seven?

"You mean the blonde one? Is she yours?"

He nods enthusiastically. "Exactly. The pretty girl. Her skin is smooth like butter. I know exactly what I'll make out of it, too. It'll make for a lovely corset. With pretty little pink ribbons to tie it together. Perfect for both style and function. And I think it'd look snazzy on display, too."

"Snazzy, yes."

How did I overlook the numbers? And who matched up to whom? Of course we haven't gotten to seven yet. Or, Emily, I think her name is. I almost feel bad that she's waiting in line on the other side. She's actually a great painter. If all Dali da Monet cared about was painting, She would be on this side of the floor, crafting away and waiting for ascension, too. But it takes more than painting to become a master of the arts worthy of the next realm.

If I'm screwing the schedule, I can screw some of the other rules as well. Dali da Monet doesn't care. Not when it comes to Dignitary status. I should be able to bend whatever I want. As long as the end result is the same, what does it matter?

"Say, what if I got you some… other materials? The freshest of them? I know they're not technically for you, but maybe you can still do something with them? I could make an exception for you."

He frowns again. "But what about the materials meant for me?"

I'll have to hurry up, make it happen faster. Make sure she's next in line even if her number isn't. But there's no time for it now. He will have to bide his time with others. Pieces meant for someone else that can share. They can share, right? It's fine. *It's fine.* "I'm sure they'll come. You just have to be patient for them. But, I'll tell you what. I like you enough that I can sneak away a few pieces of someone else's hide for you."

"And do what with them, exactly?" I know he's not trying to get on my nerves, but shouldn't this boy be thankful? I suck in a breath and hold it. No no, he's thankful. He's just curious. He really wants some advice on what to do with materials that were technically meant for someone else.

Dali da Monet, this is okay, right?

It's fine. Everything's fine.

"I don't know. Anything really. Make a belt, a lampshade, something frilly to wear. Or a wallet. The point isn't what you're doing with it. The point is to do something with it and prove to the world that art is beautiful, even in death. The point is to show them art is death and death is art and life is all of it, in the right realm."

That's right, Dali da Monet? Is that the message you want us to share? The very definition of Memento Mori.

I'm sure it is.

I'm fine. Everything's fine.

He seems to understand. "Yes, I suppose anything's possible, even if she isn't the one I was hoping for."

This is it. This is the opening I was waiting for. "You'll still get yours, Zak. If you're patient enough. Which is actually why I'm here."

I take in a breath and gather myself. Again, I'm sure Dali da Monet would be fine with this.

"Zak, what do you think is going to happen after the supermoon?"

"You and I and the rest of The Circle will ascend into the next realm, beyond reality."

"Yes. This is true. But do you believe our work is done after that? Do you really feel like the world will be saved after?"

He thinks about this for a minute then shrugs his shoulders. "I don't know. I suppose I didn't really think about it."

"Well, I have. And I don't believe the entire world can be saved at once. Not even the ones who understand their purpose. But, we can continue to recruit. We can continue to teach and lead. We can make sure that new Mori members do their part so that all artistically minded people who fully understand the depth and value of art for the sake of saving. But I can't do that from the other realm. Not in the same way someone in the realm of reality can."

"Dignitary," he swallows back. "I mean, Iris, what are you saying?"

"I'm saying I need a successor. Someone who can take my place when I'm gone from this realm. Someone who can show others how to move in the fabric of Memento Mori and continue the legacy that we're building."

His cheeks burn red. I'm sure he understands what I'm asking of him, but he won't say a word about it until I say it out loud.

"Zak, I'm asking if you would take that position."

"Me? The new Dignitary? But, why me?"

I swallow everything within me that's making me second guess if this truly is what Dali da Monet would like. Would want.

It's all absolutely fine.

"Because out of everyone else here, you have the most potential. You would know how to spot and harvest any talent. You're brash and understanding. You know how to work both a brush and a person.

You're a great storyteller, and anyone would be grateful for listening to the way you lead."

"But, I'm not ready for anything that big."

I put a hand on his knee. He's so young. There's so much he could do with the rest of his life in this reality realm.

"You're more ready than you think. Just keep meditating. Keep talking to Dali da Monet. I know you've felt Them before. It won't be long before you develop a relationship with Her like I have."

He nods. It's an acceptance. Zak is my successor. He'll take the materials I'll deliver him, from room number four, and create something with them to nurture his relationship with the ancestral artists.

It's what Dali da Monet wants, right?

I'm fine. Everything's fine.

I leave Zak's room, number seven, with damp hands and sweat. I swear I saw uncertainty in his eyes. How in the world is one woman supposed to handle all of this? All of the stress and pressure and literal weight of the world on her shoulders?

How did I do this from the beginning? How did I say jump and get No Names to ask, "How High," without a second thought? How did I do everything that requires running this whole damn operation without so much as a hair out of place? How do I make all the uncertainty in Zak's eyes and everyone else's disappear for good?

I feel so tired and run down, like I'm drowning in the necessities. If I can recreate whatever spark I had from the beginning, then maybe I can get my confidence back. It hits me. I know exactly how I'm going to get my mojo back. It'll all take place in the biggest room available.

The cafeteria.

I rush myself down there, not paying attention to any of the artists who are attempting to wave me down. Right this moment, I don't care about their lampshades and belts they're crafting. I'm sure they're great. Perfect even. Otherwise, they wouldn't have been chosen.

Unless I made a mistake.

Shit. Is it fine?

No; I can't think that way. Dali da Monet did talk to me. I heard the voices right. I'm sure we chose well.

When I get to the end of the hall, a No Name is standing there. Why is he here? Doesn't he have a job to do? No. He doesn't. I can't remember the last time I ordered out tasks. How could I make that oversight? Now every No Name on this properly is roaming around aimlessly doing what? Nothing. Nothing at all.

Shit. Shit. Shit.

I stop this man in his tracks to rectify it.

"You have a job." I try to use my most controlled voice.

"Ma'am?" As if I'm his server from a downtown diner.

"Yes. A job. I need you to gather as many workers as possible and bring them to the cafeteria."

He looks at me with confused eyes. "Go, gather. Get the job done."

I wonder if I said something that didn't make sense.

"Ma'am. Is this a job that pays?"

"What are you talking about? Of course it pays. All work you do pays out!"

His Adam's apple bobs up and down with a swallow. "I don't mean to be disagreeable, Ma'am, it's just that some of the others have been talking and, well, they think that maybe they're not actually getting paid."

I clench my jaw tight. "Excuse me?"

"No, no, not me. But I've heard others. They don't believe you have any accounts set up to pay them because they don't have access to see how much is in there."

My blood boils. This nonsense again. Of course I set them up. Of course they'll get paid. Even if it's not in monetary value, it'll be payment. I mean, a life worth saving is payment enough, right? And if they're *good* enough, they'll eventually earn their way up to serve a bigger purpose. Maybe they'll be on display themselves, their skin and bones repurposed for the sake of art. Wouldn't *that* be payment enough? To be revered for all eternity and memorialized into a one-of-a-kind sculpture?

"Well, you tell the others that sometimes there are more important things than money. But, yes, there *is* money. The accounts are all set up. And even though I've explained this thousands of times before, I'll say it again. You'll get access when Dali da Monet says it's ready. When you're able to serve your full purpose and move on into a reality that's better than this. It's all there, waiting. You just need to do your jobs to fill it up." He doesn't show that he's heard me. "Just *do. Your. Job.*"

He nods, a quiet understanding.

"Now, go. Go get the men. Make sure they come to the cafeteria as quickly as possible. After what I've just heard, I now know I have to address a *couple of* different things."

It takes twenty minutes for all the No Names to arrive in the cafeteria. At least, I think it's all of them. How many exist now? How many have I made an example of? I've lost count, but this looks like enough, I think. Maybe.

"Memento Mori staff!" My voice sounds confident enough. "I bring you here today because I realize we may not all be on the same page." Good, good. This is a good start.

"I like to think I've given you everything you need. A place to stay. Warm food. A welcoming family unit. Monetary support for when you need it later."

At my last words, there are a few mumbles that irritate my ears.

"I don't believe I've left any of you for want. And yet, here we are."

I gesture to the entire room. "I hear that some of you are unhappy. Unhappy with what? I couldn't imagine. I work my ass off to make sure you have all that you need." I suck in a breath. "I suppose some of you are living a life around believers without being a believer yourself. What it must be like to walk in the steps of a sham."

The murmurs grow. I can see some of the men whisper to another.

"So, if that's the case, maybe I need to prove the reality that we're living in. I understand I can stand in front of you all day and tell you about what I've heard and felt every time I sit down with the highest power possible."

When was the last time Dali da Monet actually came to me? I fear it's been too long. It's fine. It's fine. It's fine.

"I could recite and reiterate every word that's been told to me, but I know it won't mean anything to the non-believers."

I gather myself again.

"The thing is, we all matter here. Even each of you. Your part in this organization is imperative to running it. If you're not all in, then everything falls apart. This is why the people standing in this room today are standing here. So far, you've all done enough to prove your purpose. Anyone else has gone to dust. I want to believe you all deserve better. That your purpose will be stronger. But if you all are so damn hell-bent on getting your *money*..."

I shove my hand into my pocket where I keep a handful of change, grab a handful, and toss it into the crowd. A few of them scramble for it, but most stand stationary still. Good for them.

I know better. I know at any point in time, my ascension will come earlier than expected. These things happen. Even though the Supermoon is what will call most of us home, I'm locked in. And in case there's a toll to cross that bridge, I need to keep enough on me.

I'm The Dignitary. I won't need much. Right?

I'm fine. I'm good. I'm the high power under the high power, right?

But if these jokers think they need something now for the same reason, let them scramble for it. They'll see. Their times will come. They'll understand.

When? I'm second-guessing all of that, too.

"You see? I can see exactly who is a believer and who isn't. There are some of you who won't even flinch. To you, Dali da Monet thanks you for your service. To the rest." I look at the three or four men in the front who went for my trap. One of whom is counting the coins in his palms. Guarantee, it's less than a dollar. And yet, he's coveting it as if it's his last.

It might as well be.

"You," I point him out. "Your purpose is now. Be my example. Show the rest of these hard workers exactly what you get when you want more, past what the higher power ancestors deem necessary."

I search the room for expressions. Most of them are blank. Some appear a little more understanding. Maybe this is the time to give them a chance to showcase their own gumption.

"I need one volunteer, and sure, yes, your account will fill up tremendously." I roll my eyes, wishing to get past the concept of money. "I need someone to work the incinerator. Who will it be?"

A single hand shoots up. A Black No Name who hasn't been here long. He looks ready, determined to prove himself. Something about his face makes him familiar. He did something, right? I feel like he did something that made me not like him. But my brain can't pinpoint whatever it is.

That's okay. It's fine.

It doesn't matter what he's done in the past. All that matters is what he's willing to do now. He will help me teach this lesson nicely.

"Good. Escort this man to the crematorium. I'm sure you know what to do from there."

He makes his way over to the first man, grabs his arms, and restrains him perfectly. The first No Name pulls at his shoulders, attempting to break free. But the second No Name doesn't even flinch. His face is stone-still and his grip is vise-like. Maybe I did like him after all.

"No! No! Let go! You can't do that!" The first No Name's screams annoy my ears. I roll my eyes. What's done is done. My point's been made, and that's that.

"Let go of me, you ass! Get your hands off!"

But the second No Name doesn't let go. His grip is impressive. I don't even see his muscles strain as he walks the first man to the door.

The crowd around them breaks to make an easy path. Some look like they're holding their breath. Others have clenched fists. I wonder if those men wish they had the pleasure to escort the first man to his duty. If that's the case, they should have volunteered.

"No! No! No! Let go!" His screams are a repeated chorus I'm glad I don't have to hear for long. Each word gets softer and softer as they move out the door and on their way to the golden road of opportunity for both of them.

I smile as each of the remaining No Names turn to look at me. Some have clenched jaws. Others' eyebrows are alert. A few pursed lips tell me, they're ready to pay attention.

Stoic, nervous, ready to listen to whatever might come next.

Good. I've got my mojo back. At least temporarily.

Everything's fine.

CHAPTER TWENTY-FIVE

Livvy

"Hey, plus one. Ready to be my date tonight?" I give Mariëtte a wink. She blows me a kiss back.

"I'm ready as ever," she says. "It'll be good to put some of my training in practice." She punches the air.

I look in the mirror at the way my slacks fit my legs. Giving a squat, I feel pleased. These will do nicely. If I have to run or jump or kick some creep in the groin, I'll be able to do so. I give Mariëtte a look, too. She's wearing almost an identical pair, and she's making almost an identical squatting move. Only, she's able to bend a little further and stretch a little more. Maybe I should join her and her friends in their lessons with Doctor Crane. It sure would be nice to be able to swing a kick higher and drive a punch a little stronger.

All we've got to do now is drive out to the commune, sit in as part of an audience on some weird show they're putting on, find Mills and Stark, cause some kind of diversion, and drive us all the hell out of there. No big deal, right?

No big deal. Try telling my armpits that.

At least I've got someone who will figure things out with me as we go.

We tuck Bridget into her pen, giving her an extra strawberry snack for doing so well. Without her help, we wouldn't have had any idea as to what the invitation was laying on Stark's doorstep with my name on it. How someone delivered it to this address so quickly is beyond me, but there it was, waiting for *Miss Livvy Landon and her plus one*.

Stark's note he sent back was simple. All it said was, *Say yes*. Of course I was going to say yes. Whatever he needed, whatever he asked. But it wasn't until I saw the letter on the doorstep that I even knew what I was saying yes to.

"Ready or not, let's go." I usher Mariëtte through Stark's apartment door.

She gives me a thumbs up. "Let's rock and roll."

The drive to the commune feels empowering this time. I swear, it seems like I've made this drive a thousand times before. It's becoming more familiar to me than the actual campus I attend.

We drive in silence the entire way, but my brain can't stop spinning with question after question. I assume Mariëtte is doing the same thing I am: playing out all the what-ifs when we get there.

What if we can't find Stark? What if he can't get to Mills? What if we get caught and thrown into the same dangers anyone else in that place is in? What if we're too late?

We finally pull up to the iron gate, only this time, it looks different. It's already open. For the first time in who knows how long, it's open, ready for visitors.

"This is weird," I tell Mariëtte. "It feels wrong to just drive in. Should we?"

She shrugs her shoulders. "I don't see why not. You have the invitation, don't you?"

"In the glovebox."

She pops the glovebox open and pulls out the cream piece of paper. Printed on it is a simple invitation:

000 Blackwell Ave
March 9th, 8:00PM
Bring a Plus One

Had Stark's message back to me not hinted to look out for it, I would have completely ignored this. It would have gone straight into the trash.

"Keep that in your hand, just in case we need it as proof we're supposed to be here," I tell her as we ease the car through the gate. The sign that prevented cars from entering before is gone. In fact, in its place is an arrow, showing us which direction to go.

I quietly drive through, following the same path I remember walking with Stark before. It's narrow, but we fit, as long as we go slow and carefully. There are more arrows, showing us where to go until we get to the large round building in the middle of the commune.

There, a man in a plain canvas jumpsuit waits. I slow down, roll down the window, and put on my best smile. "Hi. We're here for the viewing today." My shaky words sound foreign to even my own ears.

"Got the invite right here!" Mariëtte shakes the paper across me so the man outside my window can see it.

He nods and points forward. "Keep going straight. Follow this path for about a mile and a half. You'll see everything set up on the left, but drive past that to make the next left turn. There, you'll find an open area reserved for parking. During the viewing, make sure all devices are turned off and put away. And, if you're interested, there will be more information later about how to tune into the public broadcast viewing in a few days. Enjoy the show, and as always, listen for the messages from the artists themselves."

I give him a thumbs up and instantly regret it. He doesn't seem like the kind of guy to appreciate such a gesture.

We follow the path, just as we're told. And at exactly a mile and a half, I do see the setup. There are already people sitting in the seats. Lights illuminate the bottom half of the stage. I imagine when everything starts, lights will brighten up the top half as well. We keep going, following the path and turning left. It doesn't take long before I see exactly where everyone else has parked. I choose a spot closest to the entrance. If we need an easy out, I want to give us the best odds.

"So, I guess we go this way to the show?" Mariëtte points to the path we followed in the car.

I shrug. "Yeah, we could do that, or," I point across the grassy area nearby, "we could cross this way as a shortcut. It might just shave off a few minutes of time and give us an idea of which direction we need to go in when it's time."

"Got it."

The night chill gets to my arms, but that's not what causes the goosebumps on my skin. The knowledge that Stark is around here somewhere, wearing the same stupid outfit as all those creepy men, is what drives all the shivers across my skin.

When we reach the scene, we find two empty seats side by side and take them. I feel Mariëtte's hand creep over to mine and she squeezes it for comfort. I squeeze back and give her a smile. "You ready for this?"

"Liv, I was born ready."

I squeeze her hand again. Thankful doesn't even begin to describe what I feel for this woman. She's become a bit of a rock when Mills disappeared from her post of grounding me. After all is said and done, we're going to need to get a bigger table at Joe's for our coffee outings.

"Ladies and gentlemen," a voice bellows over a speaker. Looking around, I see that it's coming from one of the men with a nameless name tag on. "Welcome to the first ever Memento Mori Viewing on our grounds. We can promise you interesting art pieces. Sculptures you've never seen. And even though the collection isn't quite finished yet, we'd love for you to get an up close and personal look at the newest pieces we'll be bringing out one by one.

"Keep in mind, this is a private viewing for your eyes only. In a few nights, we'll have the pleasure of broadcasting a public viewing under a gorgeous Supermoon. On that night, our entire collection will be finished and there will be a big surprise in the end. We encourage you to tune into that on our private server. At the end of our time together tonight, we will give you coded access to that. Feel free to share it with any art lover you know. As long as you believe that they, too, will appreciate the deep and meaningful messages our art has to offer.

"We have several artists who have contributed to our collection tonight. Some, in more intimate ways than others. Keep in mind, it's all delicate materials and shouldn't be touched."

He then picks up a handful of something laying on a pedestal behind him. He opens his palm and blows it out into the audience. The something scatters in the air and finds its way to my seat and Mariëtte's The dust tickles my nose and makes me sneeze.

"Consider yourselves blessed to be here. Dali da Monet declares it so!"

And with his last words, lights turn on and shine on the scene in front of us. I remember seeing the five pedestals from before, when I was here with Stark. But they look different now. I recognize the same paper mâché objects, but there are also a few clay pieces that have sort of been morphed with them, placed together as if they were supposed to belong that way. A paper mâché lion has a clay fish falling out of his mouth. A clay jug is a vase for paper mâché flowers. And the paper mâché machete is now piercing a clay butterfly. It reminds me of the game Stark played to weasel himself in here. These things don't naturally go together, but when you put them together in a new context, they become an oddly delightful piece.

Then, another man enters the staged area. He has something else in his hand. It looks like a leathered, soulless mask. It has empty eyes and the stitching around the nose and mouth makes it look like it was crafted carefully by jaggedly pre-cut pieces. Simply looking at it makes my stomach turn. Stealing a glance at Mariëtte's twisted expression, I'm sure her stomach is doing the same thing.

The man holding the mask brings it over to a paper mâché hot air balloon. There is a clay figure dangling from the basket, holding on for dear life. With careful hands, he places the mask over the rounded balloon, balancing it just right to glare down at the terrified clay man.

The audience shifts in their seats as another piece comes out. This one is a little odd. It's a lamp. Though, I imagine the lamp itself isn't what's supposed to be on display. It's probably the fleshy-colored lampshade that's been roughly sewn together. This man carefully places it on another pedestal and aims its battery-operated light at the piece in front of it. He tilts back the shade a little and all I can focus on is the way the light shines through as a red, orange glow. Similar to when I've covered up a flashlight with my hand before. Only, less lively.

"Mariëtte, I don't know if I can handle this." I try to brush off the icky feeling by rubbing my arm, but all that does is smear the dust that was blown onto me from before. I sneeze again and realize that what's on my hands smells a little like musty incense. Only, deeper and deader.

Harriet. This smells like Harriet's ashes.

Bile threatens to spill out of my mouth, but I encourage it down.

"Livvy, stay calm. I've got this, remember?" Mariëtte gives me a wink before she stands up.

I brace myself for what will happen next. Because as much of a plan as we have, we're just winging the details. I just hope whatever she has in mind will be enough.

CHAPTER TWENTY-SIX

Stark

Working the incinerator isn't exactly on my bucket list of things to do. The mere smell of this place is enough to throw my senses out of whack. My stomach feels empty and full at the same time. At any moment, I'm sure I'll lose the acid that's accumulated in it.

"Hey, what's your name?" I look at the man I guided here. I'm done making up names for these people. For once, I want to know something real. I want to make this moment, this connection *real*.

He looks at me with furrowed brows. "Wh-what do you mean?" he stammers.

"Your name. Before you were stripped of your identity, before you came to this place and decided Memento Mori was where you wanted to spend your time, you had a name. A real name. What is it?"

He bites his lip as he looks into the tiny bright orange opening. It's a small door, but just enough for a body to fit, if given the right push. I can only imagine what he's thinking. The heat that's filling the room makes my skin feel like it's melting off of me. I'm sure he's probably wondering if that's what will happen to his skin in just a few moments. Even though I don't plan on giving him that push into the fire, he's probably wondering if he'll feel it. And if Dali da Monet will save pieces of him for an afterlife worth unliving.

He's probably running through all the stories that were fed to him, and wondering if any of them are actually true or if he wasted his time trying to force himself to believe them. I know if I were facing the possible end of my life, I'd be wondering what was actually real and what I had been gaslighted to believe.

"Hey," I let go of my grip and step back from him. I realize that maybe he had been gaslit enough to erase his memory of who he used to be. "Seriously, think back. Can you remember your name?"

How long has this charade been on him? How long ago was it that he was living an entirely different life? Does he even remember what that life was? Who might have been in it? Who might be missing him right this minute? Who actually cared if he lived or died or slipped away from their grasp?

He wipes away the sweat accumulating on his forehead. A few missed drops slide down his temples, and his eyes dart left and right, I assume concerned about what might jump up to grab him if he stays still so long. His eyes stop. They focus on me. His lips curl up as if he's fighting back emotion that might accidentally boil up and spill out.

"I-I," he tries to get out. His eyes glisten with tears, but he swallows them back before they can fall. "It's... Matty."

"Matty." Simply knowing his name, his real name, a piece of his identity, drops the tension I was holding in my back. This is something that's real. This is something I can understand. This is my opening to reaching who he is at his core, helping him to remember what reality is, and what it is not.

"Matty," I repeat. "Can I ask you something?"

He nods slowly, but his eyes have fixated on that glowing orange hole.

"Matty, who are you really?"

He shakes his head, as if he doesn't understand what I'm asking. I'm not sure I expect him to understand.

"I mean, the way I see it, The Dignitary has done a pretty great job at scrubbing you clean of everything that was ever part of you. The real you. In fact, we just left an entire room filled with identical men in identical suits. Everyone's been brainwashed and wiped clean. There's no distinguishing difference between you and them, and everyone else." I try to gauge if anything I'm saying is sinking in. "It's all her, isn't it?"

"There never was any money, was there?" he asks.

I give a shrug. "I honestly have no idea. But if we're being completely honest, that doesn't matter. Even if, by some miracle, she's actually saving up all the money in the world with the intention to distribute to all the No Names she's collected, when will you get it? Do you really think she's going to open up that big iron gate and let you out with a pocket full of cash? You'd have a pocket full of cash to use… where?" My arms go wide to gesture the entirety of Memento Mori. "You can't spend any of it here."

"It's about purpose," is his response.

My jaw clenches and my fingers curl into fists. This is so frustrating. "Purpose? Do you really think your purpose in the world is to blindly follow what some crazy lady says all the way to your death?" I point to the flames living in the orange opening beside us. "Like this? You think your purpose should be to jump head first in there?"

He looks at me, anger burning in his eyes.

"Crazy lady?" he spits out "Crazy huh? She's been the one to save me. To save all of us. You should know that."

Sweat is accumulating on my own forehead now, and I wipe it clean. I have no idea how much time we have together before the inevitable happens. Before The Dignitary realizes who she let back here and bursts through the door to fix her mistake. I glance back at the incinerator door and feel the flames nearly licking my skin.

"Matty, honestly, I have no idea. I'm not going to pretend I know anything about what life you had before this place. I'm sure you had your ups and downs. I have no doubt your story is full of hurdles and heartaches. But whatever it was, however lost you were, it can't be worth losing your complete self over. There's gotta be something better. A second chance. Remember you've had ups. And there are more to look forward to in the future."

He crosses his arms, and it becomes apparent that he probably is bigger and stronger than I originally thought. As he walks toward me, I can feel his challenge, and I'm a shadow in his size.

"This *is* my second chance, bud. And who are you, huh? Who are you to come at me, trying to break my spirit, make me second guess everything I've been working so hard toward? Do you really think I would have done any of the shit I've done here if it weren't for a reason?" His words are stretched thin, his jaw tight.

I know he wants to tackle me. He might even want to throw me into that opening with full force.

I take a chance and step toward him instead. My hands find their way on his shoulders. He is strong. He could easily overtake me if he wanted. I sure hope he doesn't want to. Not really.

"Matty, you're better than this." That's all I can get out before I feel his anger and stress take over his body and feed into mine.

His arms are on my arms. My stance matches his. My muscles lock into place to keep his from overpowering me.

And all I can feel is the heat from the flames licking the inside of the incinerator.

CHAPTER TWENTY-SEVEN

The Dignitary

The test show is going well. Surprisingly well. All the trepidation I had earlier today is melting away. It's like my worries were never there to begin with and Dali da Monet has clearly tapped in and made it all better. I already checked all the tech stuff. From what I can tell, the programs are working without a hitch, and I've been assured everything is lining up to be perfect for the real deal.

The real ascension. The real golden gateway into the realm beyond reality and into a new vessel the artists of yesteryear can be proud of.

The Supermoon is right around the corner.

I have no doubt Dali da Monet would approve. Even though I never heard directly.

It's fine. Perfect even. I don't have to always have a tight grip on that connection. I can let go, right? Assume what is correct? What will work? It's absolutely perfectly fine.

But now I need to check the live portion. Reading the expressions of the audience in person will be key. The whole purpose is to reach more people in the public with the messages within the art. Are we choosing the right people to see? The non-banals who may join our cause after the first ascension? The artists who will understand and take the necessary steps to help others also understand?

I make my way across the commune, letting the bright moonlight lead the way. It's hard to believe that in just a couple of nights, the sky will be even brighter. We'll have the entire world, or at least those who deserve to see, at the edge of their seats waiting to see the truth of it all right on their screens. And with the biggest finale that could possibly be created.

Bam. Boom. Into the next realm we go!

The show is lit up, with light shining on the No Names putting together what's left of the final pieces. But I'm not worried about them. It's the audience I'm concerned about. I need to know how they're responding. Do they see it? Do they understand? Do they feel the necessity art has on our very souls?

A few people are shifting in their seats. They're craning their necks, trying to get the best view of the brilliance in front of them. Others are whispering to each other. Probably swapping descriptions of how the pieces are making them feel. A few grab hold of their neighbor's wrists and arms. I imagine transferring their energy to one another, wanting to experience Dali da Monet… even if they don't know who They are yet. Perfection.

But then one woman stands up. She weasels her way out of her seat and to the front of the crowd. At first I think she's going to do something horrible, like touch the leathered pieces and take away the magic and significance they hold. But she doesn't do that. She doesn't get too close to the pieces at all.

Relief.

Instead, she turns around and addresses the crowd, instantly killing my briefly experienced relief. "Ladies and gentlemen, I don't know what kind of shit show they think they're getting away with here."

Hot embers form in my stomach. My blood boils. A shit show? How dare she use such language to describe the perfection I've created. It is perfection, isn't it? I take a moment to suck in the pedestals myself. I'm not so sure. I see that paper mâché… what? Sword? Machete? Maybe it's not such perfection. But there I go again, down the rabbit hole of collaged negativity. I'm so tired of second-guessing myself.

I decide. It's perfection because *it has to be perfection.*

Who does this woman think she is to pass judgment on something that holds so much untainted value?

"I know, I know, art is supposed to be objective and all, but *this*?" She throws her finger to address the stage we've set up. "This is abhorrent. It's disgusting. It's completely appalling if they think this is worthy of some big show." Her hands fly to the sides of her face, and her fingers circle around in their own visual sarcasm.

I'm about to go up to her myself, give her a piece of my mind, show her what kind of "big show" we can really produce. But I'm reminded of something that Dali da Monet once told me. They said I cannot allow that part of myself to show when it counts. Not when it's around the people who matter, the artists and art lovers who make a difference. And who knows who might be in the audience who will join us in our efforts later.

So I tell myself to have patience. I don't need to correct her. Not when I've trained my many minions to do it themselves. They know, don't they? I look around at the faces of No Names spread around the stage. They're confused, frustrated, some angry. It won't take long. One or two will sweep her away and do what they want with her. I don't even care if that means throwing her into solitary or the incinerator. Though, I'd rather not a pessimistic banal mix in with the ashes of our true spirits.

"I demand, *demand*, we see something bigger, better. Something that will truly take our breaths away. Something that will move us all to our knees with real, raw emotion. I don't know about any of you, but I came here expecting a change of life experience, and this isn't it. This isn't doing it for me. And I'm willing to guess it's not doing anything for you, either."

Hold on. Maybe she's not a banal. Maybe there's something to her. I stop any lingering urges to mentally will a No Name to tackle her. Maybe she's right. Maybe there does need to be something more to this show. More what, though? I can't get any of my artists to do something on the spot. I don't have any other leathered pieces to play with myself. I'm not even caught up to the pieces that should be available to my Circle. But maybe there is something I can do. Something I can provide. Something that could be added. There's not enough dust up there anyway.

That's when I get a brilliant idea. A lightbulb goes off in my head, and I realize that maybe this entire show isn't just a test over how it might work out on Supermoon day. But maybe it's also a test of the audience themselves.

I've already appointed a successor. I can go ahead and test these people now. I can call it an interactive experience. Allow them to play with new materials they've never held before. I can show them what Memento Mori is all about.

What better way than to get immersed into it?

Materials from Number Four are already claimed. But I just sent an example down to the crematorium. And if I'm quick enough, maybe I can reroute how that example gets used. New materials just might be closer than I thought. And if this audience is as good as I think they might be, they'll be glad to get hold of anything.

Even if they're not the chosen ones.

It's fine, right?

It's fine.

CHAPTER TWENTY-EIGHT

Mills

My mind is playing tricks on me. That's the only explanation I have for Stark visiting. That couldn't have been the real him, could it? Why would Stark be here? Why would he become a Memento Mori member? To worry about me? That doesn't make any sense. He should be off, doing something crazy fun. Join a party on Deuces Street, let loose, and meet a girl or two.

That last thought has my heart jumping into my throat. Or, he should at least be behind the counter at the art supply shop. He shouldn't be here, worrying about me. That doesn't make sense.

And there's no freaking way I heard him right. Livvy? Alive? That also sounds like some kind of fever dream talking. I saw her with my own eyes. Dead, in the street, right across the dilapidated house Noland trapped me in. People don't come back from death. Not in this reality realm, anyway.

Everything in the past few months trickles into memory. Livvy. Noland. All the dead girls. Livvy. There goes my heart again, only it drops from my throat to the bottom of my stomach.

If Livvy actually is alive, even if the percentages are against it, I need to be out of this crap hole, like yesterday. If I could reach her, she'd be able to tell me what those percentages actually are, and I wouldn't be going off of my fever dream delusions.

I push myself off the ground and bang my fists on the door. "Hey!" I shout. "Hey! Let me out of here! I can't take it anymore! Open up this door and let me out!"

If the Stark-like man is out there, maybe he can hear me. Maybe he'll have the key to open up the door. Then, he'd let me out into the open and there I'd find Livvy, beaming with her award-winning smile and her perfect poof on the top of her head.

There's no answer, and when I put my ear to the metal door, I hear nothing from outside. Not even the birds are awake anymore. The Stark-like man is gone. Maybe he didn't exist in the first place.

I slink back to the makeshift bed, sinking into the pretend comfort cardboard can offer. Real or not, the Stark-like man told me to wait, right? I don't have anything else to do in here, so I guess that's what I need to do. But wait for what, exactly? Ugh. I have no idea.

So, I pull the moldy blanket on top of me, attempting to block out the frazzled thoughts I can't grasp hold of and wait. Wait for whatever it is the Stark-like man thinks I'm supposed to wait for. A sign. A signal. A knock on the door.

That's all part of the plan, right?

A bang jolts me out of my thoughts. It isn't just my mind. There really is a knock on the door. Forceful, maybe, but it is there.

Maybe that's the sign.

I bend down to the little slit to see who is there. If my mind is busy playing games on itself, who knows who or what might be waiting from the other side. The Stark-like man? A No Name? Iris Mori herself? One of those birds?

"Look, there's no time. Take it now," a frantic voice yells at me, but it's not Stark. It's not even Stark-like. The voice is too frantic and high.

A hand juts through the slit, and inside the palm is a knife stained with brownish flakes. Huh. I suppose I might have been right after all. My only guess is that those dark stains were left by Paula. You know, after she sawed off her ear as a gift to Memento Mori.

After all, that's what she said, isn't it? She had to give a piece of herself to get freedom. And so maybe this is exactly what I've been waiting on all along, a chance to give a piece of myself for my own freedom.

This could be it. My way out. Back to my art. Maybe even back to Livvy.

I take the knife from him.

"You know what to do, right?" His voice is rushed.

My eyes are too busy picturing the way this knife must have sawed through Paula's flesh to respond. I imagine it hurt for her to clip off a literal piece of herself. But how? A scratch? A rip? A tear? A burn?

"Find a gift, but do it quick. We need you," the No Name on the other side encourages me.

They need me. They *need* me.

Interesting choice of words. They didn't seem to need me when I painted that mural.

But maybe that's the point. Now that I've been separated and had the chance to reflect on my promise to this family I've been given, maybe they're ready for me to come back. Maybe they've come to the conclusion that they actually do need me, regardless of how rouge I went.

Family. That's what this is, right? The Stark-like man mentioned the word cult. But that can't be. A cult is a weird religious group, right? Where you're taught crazy things about sex and love and get married off to multiple partners, right? That's not what this feels like. We don't talk about those things at all. It's just art as life. Memento Mori feels like a group, a network, an actual family who are all doing what they believe is right.

Right?

But do *I* need *them*? I take in a deep breath to sit with that question. Do I need them?

I'm not so sure, but I do need Livvy.

And if there's any chance she's still alive, I need to get out of here to get to Livvy.

Could I do the same as Paula? Could I sacrifice a piece of myself for the greater good? I place the knife behind my ear and feel the blade pinch my skin. It's a pinching feeling now, but I'm sure in a few minutes, it'll be more like a burn. I close my eyes as I use my other hand to bend the top of my ear forward. Holding my breath, I press the blade in more. White hot pain radiates from the side of my head and into my neck. I release my breath and suck in another, preparing myself to dig in deeper with one swift move.

Ready or not, here I go. My gift. To Memento Mori. To Iris. To Dali da Monet.

To Livvy.

CHAPTER TWENTY-NINE

Stark

The door of the incineration room flies open and both Matty and I swing our heads to the sound. Our arms are clasped on top of each other, and we're both sweating from the heat and the struggle of keeping control of our own stances.

The Dignitary stands in front of us, her mouth agape and her eyes wide with eyebrows squinched. "What are you doing?" She sounds confused.

I don't blame her. She sent me to do a job and now I'm here, dancing with the enemy. Only my real enemy is in front of me. And even though he may not realize it, she's Matty's enemy, too. And the enemy of the entire damned place.

Matty and I both snag a confused look at each other, then back at her.

"Do you two even know what's happening out there? Some woman is starting a riot, demanding to see more. They want to be tested themselves. Without even fully knowing it, they want to immerse themselves in the MMS life, and I'm not one to disappoint. I want to give it to them. Now. And yet here the two of you are, doing what? Fighting over who gets to be the next materials to be put to use? Good grief, stop lollygagging!"

Matty pulls my arm closer to the open door and I grit my teeth to stand my ground. I don't want to throw him in there. That wasn't part of my plan. But if I have to in order to save myself and Mills, I will.

"Unbelievable." The Dignitary's voice goes high pitched and shaky. I've never heard her like this. Not even at her absolute worst. "I need one of you to volunteer. Make a choice." Her eyes dart around the room, grasping for something that might push one of us to do something. "Let's say it'll pay everything. Whatever's left. All of it. It all goes into your account. It'll be the last job you'll ever need to do, okay? Just volunteer to come with me. I have a treat for you, a gift. If you accept it, your body will serve a greater purpose than your soul ever could have here."

She's like a stranger tempting a child to candy.

But I'm no child, and I never believed in the fake sweetness of what's been divvied out on these grounds.

Matty and I keep our ground. I refuse to move. There's no way in hell I'm volunteering. I know what that gift is and there's no way I'm going to allow her to shove it in my face, down my throat, and on the way to whatever is waiting for me after death. And there's no way in hell I'm going to let go of Matty, either. The look I saw in his eyes tells me he will gladly throw me in the furnace and leave whatever's left of me to disappear in the wind. He's ready for whatever he believes is in the package she's selling.

Neither of us respond. I take a small glance at Matty to see if he still holds the same intention in his eyes I just saw. But there's not the same fire in his eyes anymore. It's still there, but it's somehow shifted. Determination? Confusion? Resolve? I can't get a good read of him. I'm not sure he has a read on the situation, either.

The Dignitary stomps her feet and growls between her teeth, "Are the two of you going to ruin *everything* for me? I've built up so much for myself, and the two of you are going to throw it all away. For what? There's nothing on the table for you at this point. Nothing that's better than what I have to give! *Unbelievable*! Could you imagine what Dali da Monet would have to say about this? Don't you think They would want you to work for the purpose of our organization? Volunteer what you can in the name of art and souls? This isn't about you. This is about us. This is about who we are as a family!"

I use what strength I have to inch the both of us away from the incinerator door. Matty's feet scuttle on the ground as do mine. Our dance echoes in the squeaks and scuffs our shoes make against the floor. Mentally, I try to tell myself that my shoes are part of the ground. They've glued themselves solid, connecting their soles to the tile so they can't dance like Matty's movements want them to. If I tell myself it's true, it'll become true. And if I can stay like this without losing my balance, then I'll keep the both of us away from burning alive.

"For us?" I breathe out heavily, while keeping my eyes on Matty. "For ourselves? From where I'm standing, this is all for *you* and your delusions. If you want to talk about anyone being selfish, you need to look in the mirror, *ma'am*."

"How *dare* you!" the old woman says. The hate in her eyes burns just as hot as the fire inside the furnace. I don't want to touch either of them.

"It's true. You've done everything you can to brainwash every single person here. And it's worked so far. But not anymore, *Iris*. That's your name, isn't it? Iris? Isn't that part of your identity? Your *real* identity? Don't forget that before all this mess, you were someone else. You probably had a family, friends, goals. Based on the twisted nature of everything I've seen, I bet you desired to be a real artist yourself, didn't you? You wanted to create the same way your favorite artists created. You wanted to perfect your talent and do something with yourself in this world."

The fire in her eyes deepens.

"So you created this... whatever monstrosity it is. What you considered a family in itself, a group of people who would understand your desires even more than you understand them yourself. And if you could convince an entire commune of people to go along with your plans, you'd feel useful. Like you made it. You'd feel like you finally found your purpose, and it was still through what you loved, art.

"But somewhere between before cult living and during cult living, you changed… and for the worse. You let go of your previous identity, hoping to leave it in your personal rearview mirror. Identities are funny like that. Even if you try to fabricate a new one to embody, who you are at your core will always be there. You'll always be you, Iris. No matter what you might try to convince yourself otherwise. You'll always be that scared little girl who just wants to create."

Matty's stance falters just a little. Enough for me to inch the both of us one more step away from the heat. As tight of a grip as he has on my arms, I can see his muscles are starting to shake. Whether it be from the strain of using them or the way my words might have wormed into his head, he's starting to give. I just need to hold on a little longer.

"But I bet you don't even know the names of the two men in front of you. One of which has devoted himself to even serving you. You got to him, Iris. You had him and this whole place believe in you. God knows why. You never gave who they actually are a thought because you don't care about them. You don't care about any of us. As far as you're concerned, none of our identities actually exist. Not even the men who have dedicated their lives to you. We're *people*, Iris. We're actual *people* with thoughts and feelings. We have goals. We care. We want to do art our way, too. We have purpose in this world, too. But you don't care about any of those nuances in life. You're too preoccupied with fulfilling your own delusions. Do you want to know my purpose?"

I falter, too. My own ankle loosens from under me and I have to shift my weight to try and keep myself sturdy. But it's just enough so that Matty can squeeze his fingers into my shoulder and pull me around with my back toward the burning door. I had to go off and create a monologue for myself only for him to take back the upper hand.

Digging my weight into my heels, I refuse to move further. If nothing else, this stance gives me perfect eye-to-eye contact with The Dignitary. Now I can really get to her. And if Matty is listening, I can get to him, too.

"Dali da Monet doesn't even exist. And if He, She, They, or whatever you want to call it did, I can guarantee you this. If it did exist, if that really was the name of a higher power to listen to, then it wouldn't be asking you to do all of this. There is no true higher power that wants people to kill in their name. Believing otherwise means believing in evil, not truth."

She growls at me, spittle flying into the air.

That's when I catch Matty's eyes and beg him to let go. I want him to see, to get it. I want him to be the first person in this whole place who really hears what I'm saying. Not just for my sake, but for Mills's too. He doesn't.

I have one more shot.

"When was the last time you even heard Dali da Monet? I bet it hasn't happened in some time. I've been watching you, *Dignitary*. You're falling apart. Your confidence isn't there anymore. You're losing whatever grip you had on this fabricated reality. I dare you, for once in your life, look at the man in front of you and ask him his name. Ask him who he is. You've taken away everything from him and here he is trying to turn me into dust in the name of some bullshit you created. The least you can do is get to know who he is."

Something in Matty's eyes shifts, and he loosens his grip on me even though his glare stays the same.

"It's Matty! This is Matty. Somewhere along the line you took that from him and refused to give it back. But I'm here today to tell him to take it. Love it. Remember who he is. If you really cared, prove it to him. Tell him you remember who he is."

Wet tears threaten to leak out of Matty's eyes. "It's not true, is it? Tell him it's not true. You believe in us, right? You didn't make all this up just to hurt us, did you?"

The Dignitary scoffs. "Dali da Monet-" she starts, but I can tell she doesn't know how to finish it.

"Dali da Monet," she tries again, "is… real. I've heard… I mean…"

Matty completely lets go of the grip he has on me. Everything in my body relaxes, but I tell my muscles and skeleton not to get used to it. At any point in time, he could easily try to toss me in the furnace. "You have talked to Dali da Monet, right? Don't you hear Their words every day?"

The Dignitary's mouth gapes open. She looks like a fish, bobbing for water.

"You've heard the words that show us purpose, right? You wouldn't lead us blindly, would you?"

She furiously shakes her head no.

With a gentle hand, I touch Matty's shoulder. "Matty, this isn't where you belong. This isn't where any of us belong. She's taken away everything. And if there's a piece of you at all that questions it, now is the time to do something. Take your real second chance out of here."

Within the span of a few seconds, I can see a thousand thoughts race through his head. Whatever his backstory is that got him here. Whatever he was told to feel comfortable. The questions he had that led him up to scrambling for spare change on the floor. All of the inconsistencies that have led up to right here, right now.

He nods. As do I.

We move our hands as one, each reaching for one of her shoulders. She squirms like the bug she is, and yet her face is still twisted into confusion. The time for explanations is over. I grab her left side, holding an arm in place while Matty holds her right side. I don't have to look up at him to know, the fear and revenge are both driving his moves that mirror mine. She flinches. She kicks. But this old woman isn't going anywhere our hands aren't taking her.

She drags easily, like a doll. I could easily toss her aside the same way she has verbally tossed aside so many. But I feel the current camaraderie with Matty. We're in it together, carrying the emotional weight of everyone she sucked into this commune with deceit and empty promises.

Her torso bucks, and as she does so, her coke bottle glasses fall to the floor with a *click*. Too bad. The vengeful piece of me wishes she could watch her fate in crystal clear vision. Grunts seep out of her mouth, trying to come up with words, but there's no verbal diarrhea that could convince us to stop pulling her forward, closer and closer to the fiery end in front of us.

Her fast-skidding feet roughly hold us back. Just enough to make my arms uncomfortable. So, Matty and I effortlessly work together to move from dragging her to lifting her.

Again, like a doll. A kicking, grunting, bucking doll.

"Why?" Her first word at her realization of what's about to happen. "Why do you want to damn your own souls?"

She must realize that kicking has gotten her nowhere because her body slumps in the air. And now we don't have a moving doll in our hands. We have a sack of bricks; dead weight that wants to solidify to the ground at our feet.

"Dali da-" But she doesn't finish her thought.

We don't allow that to happen.

The door is three steps ahead. Three steps away from the fate of us all.

One, her fate. Her destiny.

Two, my fate. This single decision will forever be a part of me. It's a gravity I'm willing to shoulder because of the next step we take.

Three, the fate of every single person who was sucked into this commune, including Mills. If we don't make our next move, everything will cave in on itself. Who knows what she would order these No Names to do next. And after this next move, I'm going to need to move even faster. Because who knows what these No Names will do without her, too.

"Let me answer my own question, Iris. *This* is my purpose."

And we introduce her body to the opening that's been glaring at us the entire time.

She fits perfectly inside. Even with her squirming, it's like this door was built just for her.

Flames whoosh when they realize they're being fed.

Screams fill the air like fireworks. Fire licks her skin. Both the sound and vision burn in front of us. At first, the smell reminds me of Livvy after she left the straightening iron on her hair too long. But the scent quickly burns and turns meaty.

I don't know if her screams are still playing out, or if it's just the ghost of them ringing in my ears. But with every breath I take in, I'm breathing in a complicated mass of scents. Burning relief, singed regret, and every ounce of it is a piece of Iris Mori melting away.

Not The Dignitary. That was never her identity.

My stomach ties itself into knots.

We just opened the door for all of the second chances. No one else in this cult will ever have to feel trapped again.

CHAPTER THIRTY

Mills

Bang.

The unit I'm in shakes and the knife drops from my hand. *Bang. Thud.*

It clinks on the floor, the back of my ear relieved it's no longer pressing into skin. My heart doesn't know if it should be relieved or angry, so it settles on confused.

Bang, bang.

I have to sturdy myself by holding onto the walls. What the heck is that?

I crouch to the ground and again look out the slit of the door. At first, I see nothing. The moonlight shines against the pine needles of the trees in my eyesight. The Supermoon is soon. If I'm going to get out of here and make it in time, then I need to give a gift of myself. Right? I wonder what would happen if I didn't give a gift. Would Dali da Monet still approve? Or would I end up rotting away on the realm of reality?

Another slap hits the door, and two eyes stare back at me.

And this time, I'm sure of what I see.

It's Stark. Not a Stark-like man, but Stark himself. In the flesh. Here. My mind wasn't playing tricks on me at all. Just my heart.

"Mills. Mills! Are you okay?" His voice is liquid gold.

"Yeah. Yeah. I'm fine." Confused, shaken, a little unsure, but I'm fine.

He audibly exhales, and even in the dark, the moonlight is still strong enough for me to see a bead of sweat roll down the side of his nose. Ugh. I can smell the stress steaming off him.

"Are you okay?" I ask him.

He laughs. "Yeah, I'm fine, but I'll be better once you're out of there." He takes a pause and I can hear how heavy his breath is. "I found Livvy. She's with everyone else by the mock show. That wild friend of yours is with her, causing one heck of a scene. We're all ready for you, Mills. Look, stand back will you? I'm going to see if I can break the hinges."

Wild friend? After everything I've seen and heard, I'm not even sure what wild means anymore. I don't have a bar that can even judge it. So I do the only thing I can think to do. I nod, even without knowing if he can see it, and back up as far as I can.

Stark. The real Stark is here. And if I can remember the way his shoulders sit broad and strong, then I can only imagine what he plans to do with them against the other side of the door. I crawl onto my makeshift bed and curl into a ball to wait for Stark's impact.

Bang. Everything shakes.

Bang. Even though I want to run to the little slit and watch him pummel the locked opening, I try to hold myself still and in place.

Bang. I keep hoping the hinges will burst apart and I'll feel the evening air on my face. Then, I'd be able to know for sure if all of this is an elaborate fever dream or if Stark has decided to be some kind of knight in shining linen jumpsuit.

Bang. But it doesn't happen. The hinges don't break. The door doesn't swing open. The night air doesn't hit any part of my skin. And Stark is still standing on the other side, without me in his arms.

Damn it. Doing things this way is useless.

"Stark," I whisper. But he doesn't hear me.

Bang. Bang.

He keeps throwing his weight to the door.

Bang.

"Stark!" I yell.

Finally, the banging and rocking stops.

"Hang on, Mills." Stark sounds wheezy and out of breath. "I promised I'd get you out of there and come Hell or high water, I'm going to keep my promise to you."

When I step off my cardboard bed, my foot hits something metal. "Wait just a minute. I might have something that can help." I scramble to the floor and use my hands to search around. I find the knife and poke the handle out of the door opening. "Here, try this. Maybe you can loosen the hinges or something with it."

"Mills, I could kiss you."

My cheeks heat up and goosebumps run the length of my arms. I whisper only loud enough for me to hear, "Later."

He grabs the knife from me, and I back up once again. My eyes follow metal sounds from the top of the door. At first, it's fidgety, a few ticks and scrapes. There are also a few whispered swear words when I assume the knife slips from the divots in the screws. When there's an audible *pop*, relief washes over me. It's actually working. I mean, I knew it would, but watching it happen in real-time makes my entire body both tingle and relax. And even though I can't see his body react, I can hear it in his muffled grunts; Stark is relieved, too.

The metal-on-metal sounds creep down the door a little further.

Pop.

He's toward the middle, using the ear-cutting knife to find each little screw and unwinding it to the point of release.

When there's another pop, the sounds move again. And again. Each time, a buzz runs through me.

Pop. Pop. Crash.

The door breaks free and flings open, only a deadbolt lock holding it in place.

A bit of linen is in an awkward lump on the ground. Perhaps that's the No Name who fed me the knife in the first place. The first bangs I heard must have come from Stark's fist and his face. The moonlight shines on the lump in a way where I can only make out the outline. I assume he's still breathing, but the way that body is laying there, I also assume it's going to be a while before he opens his eyes and pieces together what happened while he was knocked out.

Reality is setting in. Stark really did come for me. And not just for me in the way that every other No Name in this place came for me. He came for me on very different terms. So that I can be free. Out of solitary, and out of the grasp this place has intricately wrapped around me.

My glance moves from the body on the ground to the body in front of me. Stark. Stark's body.

We lock eyes for a moment, then in a quick moment, he rushes to me, throws his arms around my waist, and pulls my body into his. He holds me tight against his torso. Never before have I felt Stark's touch. He's never held me like this, but it feels like home to be in his arms, so I throw my arms around him and hug him just as tight.

"I'm so glad you're okay," his deep voice whispers in my ear.

All I can do in response is to hold him even tighter, which doesn't even seem possible, but I do anyway.

He sucks in a breath and lets it out in my ear. "I hope your legs are ready because we're going to have to run. Okay?"

I whisper back into his ear, "I've never been more ready to run away than I am now."

CHAPTER THIRTY-ONE

Livvy

Mariëtte is one of those people who you never know what's hidden beneath the surface. I have to literally close my gaping mouth with my own hand while watching her in front of this crowd. She has every person's eyes locked on her. Some people are shouting back, telling her to get off the stage and leave for the real entertainment to take place. Others whisper, making assumptions as to who she is and guessing if her identity has anything to do with art itself. Some even wonder if she's the person who actually sent out the invitations in the first place. And still others are clapping as if she's the show's main event.

People are weird and unpredictable.

I've never seen so many confused men and women collected in one place, but here we are. Every single one of them has a different assumption to make on the girl in front of them. And Mariëtte Dunn has the attention of every single pair of eyes, providing the exact distraction Stark and I need.

I had caught a glimpse of him, running toward the trees and toward who knows what. I'm assuming he's off to get Mills. Once he does, I know we'll have limited time. Everything will have to happen quickly and without a second thought. So I know it won't be long before I'll need to grab Mariëtte, Mills, Stark, and the car and race out of here. I hope she can keep the crowd's attention for a little longer to stir the pot enough.

In her biggest voice, she announces that this is a joke, the whole show is a sham and not worth the time it took to travel here. I hold my breath, sure her words will kick off a riot. A riot would be the perfect distraction.

Lucky stars, it happens.

Within seconds, the boo-ers stand up and scream back at her. "Proof that women don't know shit!" one man yells. "Stay home if you're on your period. Don't bother the rest of us with your bullshit."

A woman near him smacks the man in the back of his head. "And you're proof that men are butthurt babies who can't walk away without getting all emotional over a woman's opinion." She yells out to Mariëtte, "Go on, honey. You say what you need to."

Mariëtte gives her a wink. Had she not been on a mission, I'm sure she would have pulled that woman aside and asked her stories of how she's supported the women in her own circle.

A few of the whisperers get louder. "Is this part of the show or are we getting jipped?"

"Yeah, who the hell are you?"

"I bet she's one of those new-age protestors."

"I thought we came here to see some artwork. The eff is all this?"

"Someone get her before she starts supergluing her hands on the artwork and yelling about pollution or something stupid like that!"

And one even starts yelling at the yellers to calm down so they can better hear what's happening.

One by one, everyone in the audience gets up in their seats. The angry man locks eyes with Mariëtte. He starts to make his way toward her. His eyes nearly glow red with fury, like he's going to tackle her for simply existing in his presence.

The woman who hit him grabs hold of the back of his shirt to pull him back on his heels. She pulls back her arm and hits him again. He stumbles backward, knocking over one of the chairs that falls on top of another woman's leg.

"Ow!" she yells. She turns to the person next to her and shoves them. "Why'd you do that?" It only takes seconds before fists are flying in every direction. It's difficult for me to know where one arm begins and the next ends. It's like being in the middle of a flesh-and-nail tornado, and somehow I got cast as the calm eye in the storm.

There's a small opening near me, just a few seats over where no one's fists are hitting anyone else.

Mariëtte's voice is still carrying through the chaos. I hear the words "more" and "show off" and I think the last one is "better," but it could have been "bullshit."

I duck to avoid a lady's fingernails clawing at the air around me.

She ends up scratching someone else's arm.

I dodge another attack, a thrown shoe. A stiletto heel that matches the red dress of the woman scrambling on the ground next to me.

And once I get close to my opening to freedom, I get a glimpse at Mariëtte. She's enjoying it. She's doing a dance of words and accusations, stirring up the tornado she created.

Something jabs my side. It forces the wind out of my lungs with radiating pain in my ribs.

"Damn it!" I double over just in time to roll away from a second attempt from the elbow that caused it.

Finally, I reach my goal. I'm out of the crowd, on the sidelines, equally impressed and terrified as to how quickly a few chosen words caused such pandemonium.

This might make for a more interesting paper than bunny oxytocin.

Mariëtte throws her hands into the air and says, "Open your eyes and see what's really going on here. If you think this," she circles her hands behind her, "was created for you to ooh and ahh over, you're deadly wrong. *Deadly*. There's something much bigger going on, much-"

One of the men participating in the event drops the leathery thing he had been holding and charges toward Mariëtte. I think he's going to knock her down, but she sees him coming. Mariëtte plants her feet to the ground, steadies her arms, and grabs hold of the man before he can grab her.

She crouches. Using the force he charged her with, she catches him and flips him over her head.

The crowd gasps.

The tornado pauses.

Misogyny Man looks like he's going to join the man for backup. Feminist Woman pulls a phone out of her clutch and brings it to her ear. I assume she's calling the police. And in the same breath, Mariëtte pivots herself to pin the man to the ground.

It's probably a good thing the police are being called. Here in a few minutes, we'll be home free and they can take care of whatever mess is left behind.

Scrambling underneath Mariëtte, the man kicks his legs like an angry octopus. A lucky kick knocks her off, and he rolls to his side to stand back up.

The two of them stare each other down. For a few extended moments, they're the eye of the storm. They're the calm that calms everything down.

But then the squall picks up again. He moves left, but she moves left quicker. He leans right and she's prepared. He lunges forward and she dodges as if she knows exactly what move he takes before he takes it.

Her training has clearly paid off.

While the crowd is yelling and screaming, some questionable people taking sides of the man, others rooting for Mariëtte to finish him off, something catches the corner of my eye. A bright light. Headlights. A horn blares as the car runs across the grass and approaches the crowd. Our ride out of this mess and into the safety of the reality this entire place forgot existed.

It skids to a stop, just a feet away from the commotion.

"Liv, get in!" Stark shouts from the window. My heart rate increases to double time.

"Mariëtte!" I yell to her, though I'm not sure she can hear me above the crowd. "Mariëtte!"

She gives me a quick thumbs up to say she does, then in a flash, her fist finds itself in the man's throat. I catch her quick laughter, and give a chuckle, too. Both his hands grab where she hit as he tumbles to the ground. She waves goodbye to him from her stance above, then she books tail to the car before anyone in the audience can catch up to what's happened.

We both slip in and slam the doors behind us.

Stark slams on the gas and takes the drive back out of the Memento Mori commune for, what I hope, is the last time for all of us.

I turn to the person next to me. There are a thousand things I want to say. Probably a million I want to ask. But all of that can wait. I throw my entire weight onto her. "Mills! You're alive!"

She hits me on the arm before squeezing me back, "And so are you!"

CHAPTER THIRTY-TWO

Livvy

A few days later

"So, you're telling me that a rabbit told you how to break your friend out of this…"

"Commune, sir."

The look on Officer Fuzz's face tells me that he's trying to hold it in. He doesn't want to appear shocked, but clearly even in the law force, he hasn't yet seen it all.

I uncross and recross my legs. Hospital benches aren't exactly the most comfortable. Even less so when police decide to question you and your friends about insane cult stuff. "And, no, she didn't tell me how to break her out. She just delivered a message to my brother and brought a message back."

He scratches at his chin, I assume mentally checking his notes. "Your brother, who posed as a member of this cult?"

"Yes, sir."

"And how exactly did you get this rabbit to deliver messages back and forth?"

I pucker up my lips and give him a little "Wheet-woo" whistle, then followed up with a wink.

Officer Fuzz chuckles. "Well, that's a first for me. Okay then. Tell me what happened."

I explain everything I can to him. Everything from when Stark and I first arrived on the commune grounds, how everything was so pristine and pretty, it was the perfect mask. It all appeared nice and pretty on the outside, but how it was run and who was running it made it rotten to the core. Beeping machines provide background music to the details I'm able to give him, and I kind of wish Mills and I could give our versions of the story together. But, I suppose, that's exactly why he asked if he could see me separately. To keep our versions our own without their details doing any unintentional weaving.

"They even sent out invitations to a creepy art show where they showed off some of the art pieces that are… unsettling at the least." I stop talking. It dawns on me. "There were a bunch of people there, too. I'm sure they'd be great witnesses to question if you can find them!"

Fuzz holds his hands up. "Thank you, Ms. Landon, but we've already got our men on it. It'll take a while, but we're going to make sure we get statements from everyone we can. You just focus on yours, okay?"

I nod. "Yes, sir. I think I've given you everything I can."

"In your words, you say the person or people who was running the place was 'rotten to the core.' Can you elaborate on that?"

"I could, sir, but I think my brother could give you a better description of that."

***

Stark

Officer Fuzz's pen taps on the table in front of me. *Tap tap tap tap tap tap tap*. The continuous noise would bother me in any other situation, but I know he's just trying to take it all in. I can't imagine how many notes he's already recorded. I can only imagine how many of the hundreds of survivors might want to tell their stories, as the witnesses of the trial show.

190

The more he taps his pen on this tiny table, the more I wish the nurse would come back to me. I know I'm not hurt, but it might be nice having another person in the room. Someone who can at least make sure I'm safe if I tell this man exactly what happened.

"Can you tell me again about the uh-" Fuzz flips his paper back and forth, looking for the right name for the person who put us all through this hell.

"The Dignitary?" I hold my breath, unsure if he believes the story I'm telling him. His face tells me nothing, and he hasn't verbally given me any clues as to what he's heard from either Livvy or Mills.

"Yes, The Dignitary. You said she's who gave all the orders to the-?" He leaves the question hanging.

"No Names, sir."

"Right. The No Names. And they are-?"

I give a sigh because I know it's all coming down to what he knows I did. And if I say it out loud, I'm sure my future will be much more complicated. "They're the workers there. She was the powerhouse of the whole operation, and somehow, she convinced them all that what they were doing was… a good thing." My voice trails off, replaying the horror I endured while pretending to be a part of it all, willingly.

He scratches at his bristly beard. "Things like?"

Even though I'm getting tired of his hanging questions, I still answer them. "Sir, unspeakable things. Like being a part of the brainwashing. Disassembling human corpses. And, um" I look him in the eyes. There's a kindness to them. An understanding. Even though he's probably not supposed to sympathize with what I'm about to say, I get the feeling that he knows something that might just hit his compassionate side. "And murder."

I expect his eyes to widen, his face to drop, but his eyes still read hopeful. "And did you participate in any of the murder?"

I don't want to say yes. I don't want to admit my hands did such a horrible thing. But honesty is the best policy, so I nod.

He puts down his pen and clasps his hands together. "I see," he says. "And again, it was-?"

"The Dignitary."

"That's exactly what I thought."

"Sir." I know he has questions, and I know I hold some of those answers. So before he can ask me anything else that just needs filling in, I decide to let it all out and beat him to the punch. "She had such a grasp on everyone. Literally everyone. She could tell any one of her cult members to do the worst she could imagine, and they believed it was good. I can't explain why or how or what any of them were thinking. Other than, they thought it was right, that the deity they believed in wanted them to. Just because she said so."

I suck in a deep breath before I continue. "And even though they were devoted to her and her orders, she did the same to them, whenever she felt like it."

"The same what?" he asks for clarification.

"Sir, she would murder them, too. If she felt like it was called for, she murdered them, too."

He leans back in the chair some more. From the cracked opening of the room door, I see a face. The nurse who had checked in with me before. I smile at her, and she waves back. But since she sees Fuzz with me, she backs off and walks away. She's probably waiting for him to leave so she can discharge me. Harm free, and ready to go.

The damage is done anyway. I've already told him. He may have even made up his decision already.

"So she murdered the - uh - No Names?" I can tell he's struggling to recall the hierarchy of this cult.

I nod my head. "Yes; the No Names. And the artists. I imagine she would have with the people who came for her show, too, if she could have figured out how to do so undetected. No one was safe from her."

"How about you? Were you safe from her?"

I hang my head. "Sir, it was kill or be killed. I know it was wrong. Murder should never be the solution. But in that moment, when an incinerator was just feet away and a gaslighting cult leader was in our path, we would have been thrown in if we didn't do it to her ourselves."

"We?"

Crap, I didn't mean to bring Matty in this. But here we are. "Yes, sir. His name was Matty. I don't know a last name. But, please, this was my idea. All me. He just happened to be there, just as confused as ever over what's up and what's down. Right and wrong were so mixed up in his head because of her. And if we didn't do it, I'm sure she would have gone after others. So many others. Others like, others like…"

It's his turn to fill in the blank. "Like your friend."

Again, I nod.

Officer Fuzz adjusts in his chair. Something changes in his posture. The understanding in his eyes melts into the rest of him.

"Look," he starts, "off the record, I'm not going to pretend like I know what it was like being there. I imagine what you saw during your time at this commune will probably sit with you for the rest of your life. For that, I am sorry."

He adjusts in his seat again. "On the record, I can tell you that we have had our suspicions about this place and the people in it for a while. Some of us have considered the possibility of the murders around Volga University being connected somehow. But we never really had any proof to go off of. Fortunately, and unfortunately, this is the exact type of thing that needed to happen for us to move forward on an investigation."

He scrunches up his eyebrows for a moment, then releases them. "Off the record again, I can see your moral dilemma here. And while I can't promise that this is the last time you'll have to answer questions regarding this, I can tell you one thing. You have a great case for self-defense. And with the amount of witnesses we have giving statements, I'm sure it wouldn't be too hard for that to stick."

***

Mills

Cold shivers run through my body, but it's not uncomfortable. It's making me feel more awake. And clear-headed. I don't remember the last time a clear thought ran through my head. Man, IV hydration fluid is somethin' else.

I wish Livvy were here. I want to know everything. I want to hear how she got away from Noland, found where I was, and got her brother to agree to fake devotion to a weird art religion that was somehow starting to make sense to me.

Ugh, I feel dumb. How could I have ever believed that stupid man was a good mentor for me?

There's a knock on the door. For a minute, I get the best-friend tingles. And just as quickly, they run away. Some cop is helping himself into my room.

"Emily Ellis?" he asks. And for the first time in a long time, I don't get angry hearing my full name. I suppose I'm feeling more like myself. Name or Nickname doesn't matter.

"That's my name, don't wear it out!"

He chuckles. It feels good to make that happen.

"Can I get you a cup of coffee? Water?"

I consider it for a moment, but shake my head. I can smell the coffee on his breath, and I get the feeling whatever the hospital has in their waiting rooms just isn't quite my usual at Joe's. Pretty sure it's a knockoff, boring brand I want nothing to do with. But, I'm being kind, so I don't say anything. I just shake my head no and tell him I'm ready to start when he is. I already know he's gonna ask me questions. And I already know I'm gonna want to get this over with *asap*. So, I don't even wait. I dive in. Straight from the beginning and with as few pauses as I can manage. The sooner I get outta here, the sooner I can see Livvy and Stark.

And get a good cup of Joe's that doesn't smell like ass.

I tell him everything, doing my best not to skip any important details. When I do, I stop, rewind, and try again. I tell him what I believed and didn't. I tell him about Noland's cleansing baths and how they starved recruits to help brainwash us. I tell him about everything I knew and about all the people I got to know, even if it wasn't through conversations or names or anything like that.

I tell him about Paula and Zak. About all the No Names who were there. I tell him about Iris Mori. Then, I tell him about the different crafts we were told to create.

And when I get to the end, telling him about solitary confinement and breaking out, I'm out of breath.

"And, I think that's it," I finish, and I'm about ready to go. I want to push myself up and out of this room, rip out this IV, skip out to my friends, and celebrate with coffee.

But Officer Fuzz has other ideas.

"Well, that's quite a story there, Ms. Ellis."

"Yup! And, well, it's all true. Every bit!" I want to dust off my hands and be done with it all.

"That, I have no doubt. I've talked to a lot of people, Ms. Mills. And it all matches up. As horrible and awful as it all seems, there's nothing you've said that makes me think you're embellishing anything."

"Yeah," I bite my lip. "Yeah, unfortunately, I'm not."

Paula's face flashes in my memory. Her strawberry red hair framing her face, and her kind eyes that never wanted to fully look up. A lump catches in my throat. Stark told me what happened. And as mixed up as I was, and if I'm being honest, still might be, she didn't deserve to die like that.

The world should have seen what her artistic mind could do.

I make a mental note to look her up. The internet is great for cataloging the accomplishments of people. I'm sure I'll be able to find at least a few photos of what she's done before.

But what about the others? What about all the No Names who lost themselves? Will they ever find their way back to their identities again? What about the other artists who never got to fully express themselves? What about Zak?

"Officer Fuzz," I start.

"Hm?" He pushes his chin forward and gives me a look that tells me he's listening with his whole self.

"What about all the survivors? What's going to happen to all the people who were a part of Memento Mori? Will they be okay?"

He gives me a quiet smile, and nods. "There's no getting around it. Living through an experience like you did is hard. Some people are going to have a hard time being okay. Some are going to have a really hard time. But I have no doubt, with a supportive group of friends like the ones you have, you'll be okay."

Zak's face drifts into my mind, and I shake my head. "Not everyone has that, though. Will they be okay?"

Fuzz's smile quietens a little more. "I can't guarantee anything, but I can say this. After knowing what happened on the Blackwell grounds, we are shutting it all down. The county is taking over the property. Everything will be torn down and rebuilt into maybe a park, a garden, a community center… who knows. And as far as the people themselves, well, we work closely with a group of therapists in Volga County. Even though we can't dive into all the details with them yet, word has spread. They've reached out. And I know for sure they are willing to help any one of the people who were a part of this ordeal as best as they can."

I nod. "I suppose that's all anyone can ask for, right? The offer of help. I'm glad there are professionals willing to help."

He leans forward, with one hand flat on the table. "And they're willing to help you, too, Emily. I have the name of a therapist I think would work really well with you."

I roll my eyes, even though I'm incredibly thankful, knowing a therapist is probably exactly what I need. "I guess I have one more person to drag down the rabbit hole, huh?"

"I suppose you could say that."

CHAPTER THIRTY-THREE

Mills

The Next Day

Bridget's little nose tickles my hand. For an overgrown furry rodent, she sure is cute. "So this is the critter that saved my life, huh?"

"Nah. This is the critter that saved your life." Livvy nudges Stark's arm. She still hasn't given it a rest. Me and Stark. Together. As if it was her plan all along. If that's the case, she's an evil mastermind. And considering how he and I really aren't together-

Not yet.

-she's not that great as a matchmaker mastermind.

"Hey!" he calls back.

"What? It's true."

My cheeks turn hot. Not that I mind the idea. It's not every day a man will infiltrate some insanely art-religious cult to save my life.

And even though she's always said she'd do it, it's not every day my best friend provides a getaway car to safety. "Eh, Liv, don't deny it. You're also a critter who helped."

"And Mariëtte!" Livvy reminds me.

"And Mariëtte," I repeat. Who would have thought a crazy sorority girl would have played a part in it, too. "You all are some kind of stupid for putting yourself in danger like that."

"Stupid is as stupid does," Livvy hits back. "Besides, you really think we'd leave you there alone?"

I pick up Bridget and give her a little nuzzle. "In fairness, I thought you were dead, Liv. And you…" I look up at Stark and feel my cheeks redden again. I hope it's not obvious. "I would have never pegged you as a spy."

He scratches the back of his neck, trying to hide the coy look on his face. "Well, I kind of had to. You see, there's this thing I need you to do for me that I really can't ask of anyone else. It'd be too awkward."

I cock my eyebrows. Oh no. Not now. Not here. Is he really going to do this now, in front of his sister? I'll never hear the end of all the, "I told you so's," that are brewing within her.

"You see, there's this thing that just doesn't feel right, not without your hand on it."

Gulp.

"Ew!" Livvy shouts from the couch. "The heck, Stark? Couldn't you wait until I'm gone for that? And then never say those words in public again."

My thoughts exactly. Maybe behind doors I could respond a little better, but here? In his living room? With his sister watching? Excuse me?

Stark rolls his eyes. "Hold on," he tells us both as he leaves the room.

Confusion rolls over me, and I look to Livvy for answers. A shrug tells me she doesn't have any.

My breath hitches in my throat when he comes back. "Is that…?"

"Yup. It's your painting. At least, I'm pretty sure it's yours, right?"

I look at my self-portrait. The one Noland made me create. The one that showed how trapped I felt, and how trapped I really ended up being. I give him a nod. "Yeah. Yeah; that's mine." A lump forms in my throat. I don't know how he ended up with it in his possession.

"But you see this here?" He points at Noland's signature in the corner. "That's not you. So, Emily Ellis, I'd like to ask you a favor. Would you do the honors of rectifying this? So you can take back ownership as the rightful artist?"

He hands me a paintbrush. Just a regular paintbrush he probably got from the local craft store. Nothing special about it. Nothing other than it came from Stark. Which makes it absolutely perfect. From this point on, I'm only painting with brushes like this. Then, he dips it in black paint. Just regular black paint without any presumptuous name attached to it. Also perfection.

I gladly take it and cover up Noland's wimpy signature with my own bold one.

Done. That creep and his whole gang of monsters are wiped out forever.

EPILOGUE

Mills

"You know, there is nothing that compares to good coffee." I take another sip of my cup of black Joe's. I can feel the caffeine take a little trip through my veins, waking up every bit of me in bitter warmth. "Tea just doesn't have the same effect."

"You've got that right." Stark takes a sip of his own dark roast coffee.

As many times as I've sat in Joe's with a cup to drink, I don't think I've ever sat across from Stark. Alone. On a date.

It's weird.

But the good kind of weird.

I'm definitely learning the difference between the good and bad kind, and I'm all about the kind that makes me feel comfortable right away like Stark has always done.

"So, who's turn is it now?" I ask him, glancing down at the napkin between us. It's folded back in several places. Neither of us can see what's on the other side, and I only know what's hidden on half of those folded slots.

"Oh, it's definitely mine. Hand me that pen." Stark opens up his palm for me to put the pen we're sharing into it.

He accepts the pen, then sticks out his tongue. He bites down on it as he puts the ink to the napkin while his other hand hides the marks he's making.

I always knew Stark had a creative bone hidden somewhere in him. But I never had the chance to actually see it for myself. I suppose doing something nonchalant like joining a cult can actually make you remember things about yourself. Things that were once hidden and need to be brought to the surface.

"Here." He folds the napkin back and hands both it and the pen to me. "Now you go."

I take it back and see what's left. There isn't too much room to do anything else. Just a cramped space big enough to add something teensy to the bottom of our collaborative drawing. I put the end of the pen to my chin to think. The heck will go in that spot that will make sense? Not that anything actually will. It's all for kicks and giggles anyway. Our own majestic corpse. Though, I think I might prefer calling it something like… exquisite telephone.

Stark's smile pulls my attention away, as does the tapping his foot gives me under the table. "Stop it! How am I supposed to function as an artist if you're going to be distracting like that?"

"Function as an artist?" He laughs. "Mills, you'll never not be an artist." He links his fingers into mine. The way his dark skin interlocks with my pale fingers makes my heart jump with flutters. "Just think of it as inspiration, not a distraction."

My tongue sticks out of my mouth. What a dork.

A cute dork.

Ugh. My heart doesn't want to stop bouncing.

But then it does. It stops altogether, and I pull my tongue back in.

Two eyes catch mine from behind Stark. A face I never thought I'd see again. My stomach flips. And this time, not in a feel-good way. He looks up from his drink. Waves. And stands up to head his way to our table.

"Zak?" I say, but my stupid mind is wiped clear of anything else.

"Hello, Mills." The way his lips turn up at the corners is the same. But I don't remember the way his smile doesn't reach his eyes. "It's good to see your pretty face."

Stark gives me a scowling look. I want to tell him he has nothing to worry about. It's not like I'm Zak's type. At all. But the words catch in my throat and I can't explain why.

"I see you're busy, so I'll keep it short."

Zak adjusts the strap on his shoulder. My eyes follow the strap down to the bag it's attached to. I hadn't noticed it until now. The leather computer bag. It looks just like all the others that come in and out of Joe's. Just another kid toting around another laptop for a term paper or research or to track down the people that should be lost within their personal histories forever.

Only, it's not the same. The patchwork stitching looks more handmade than mass-produced. And the stitches are dyed strawberry red. The same shade as Paula's hair.

He pats the bag carefully, and that same awful smile drags across his face again.

Then, he leans over the table, with his elbow covering our doodle napkin. I can smell the sugar on his breath from his junk coffee as he says, "It should have been you."

A REVIEW REQUEST

Thank you so much for dedicating some of your time to get to know the characters who have been with me for so long. If you enjoyed this book, please take a few minutes to rate and review Paint by Murders on Goodreads or Amazon.

Even a few words help others decide if this is the book meant for them.

Your Book is Lonely!

Please consider adding a few friends on your shelf!

<u>Emily Ellis Thrillers</u>
Paint by Murders
Paper Machete
Majestic Corpse

<u>Other Books by Amanda Jaeger</u>
The Fallen in Soura Heights
BreathTaken

ABOUT THE AUTHOR

Amanda Jaeger: Murderino mom of two, professional word nerd by day and author by trade.

She's the wife of her college sweetheart, and the mother of two spit-fire girls, but she's also been a sign language interpreter, transcriptionist, and a book slinger. Working with words isn't her job, it's her career.

Thank goodness writing thrillers come naturally to her.

Amanda refuses to start her day without the perfect cup of coffee and a cuddle with her poodles. She also wants to let you know that poodles aren't as prissy as they seem, and they are, in fact, made of teeth, nails, and heads as hard as steel.

Residing in Virginia, you can bet on Amanda listening to true crime podcasts, watching cold case documentaries, and playing with her kids. (Not simultaneously).

And even though Amanda kinda sucks at keeping up with social media trends, she loves connecting one-on-one with readers.

You can connect with Amanda:

Text "ThrillerRead" to: (844) 495-1120

ACKNOWLEDGMENTS

Holy crap I hope I don't forget anyone. It takes a village, yall. It's just as true for paperback babies as it is for the real life sticky ones. (And yes, kids are sticky.) So please bear with me and if you made it this far in this book, then keep on reading. These are my village to have helped make this trilogy the crazy semi-beast it is.

Before I head into it, let me clear the air that ALL MISTAKES ARE MIIIINE.

Hey YOU, yes you. The person reading this. Thank YOU. You're the reason why I write and continue to write. The characters and stories may start with me, but you're what keep them alive for much, much longer.

To the real life Mariëtte who really is one of those people who you never know what's hidden beneath the surface. Thank you for being my number 1 Alpha. You're always there to help me find the gaps when my brain is fried. And without you, I'd probably get every forensic scene 1,000% wrong.

To allllll the betas: Anna, Danielle, Jamie, Carmen, and Sam. Thank you for helping me refine the details, close the gaps even further, and sometimes rearranging the cluster in my head to make more sense on paper.

The Thriller Babes: You know who you are. Out of the entire writers community, you are the pillar that keeps me standing when the frustrations run high. Your help, guidance, expertise, and self-deprecating memes are everything I ever wanted in a peer mentorship. Thank you!

My editor, Genevieve… good grief I couldn't do this without you. Thank you so much for helping me clean things up as I learn and relearn what the heck grammar is all about. (You'd think as an English major I would have had some kind of grammar class… but nah."

Troy! You're stuck with me. Forever. Deal with it. Thank you for always knowing exactly how to take my insane descriptions and translate them into visuals. I know they say "Don't judge a book by its cover," but we all know that's the first thing people judge a book by. Your cover designs make my first impressions better.

To my husband, Michael, for always being supportive of my crazy writing "hobby" (slash work slash obsession). Because of you, I have the time, space, and love to actually create the stories that keep me up all night.

My kids, who keep asking what the heck I'm writing about but aren't allowed to yet read it. I know you two have snuck a few peeks over my shoulder. I'm not mad, but I'll definitely understand if you need therapy later. Love you to pieces.

And the rest of my family who continue to be supportive both loudly and quietly. Thank you for reading when you want, loving me even when you don't want to read it, and smiling when I talk to much about it. THANK YOU FOR BEING YOU.